SLAY RIDE

A SAMANTHA KIDD MYSTERY

SLAY RIDE (LARGE PRINT EDITION)

Book 10 in the Samantha Kidd Mystery Series

A Polyester Press Mystery

This Large Print edition is unabridged.

First published 2019

ISBN: 9781954579712

SLAY RIDE

A SAMANTHA KIDD MYSTERY

DIANE VALLERE

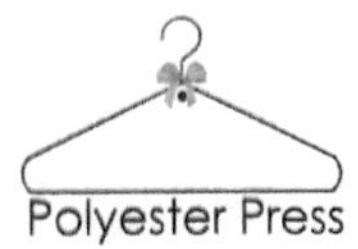
Polyester Press

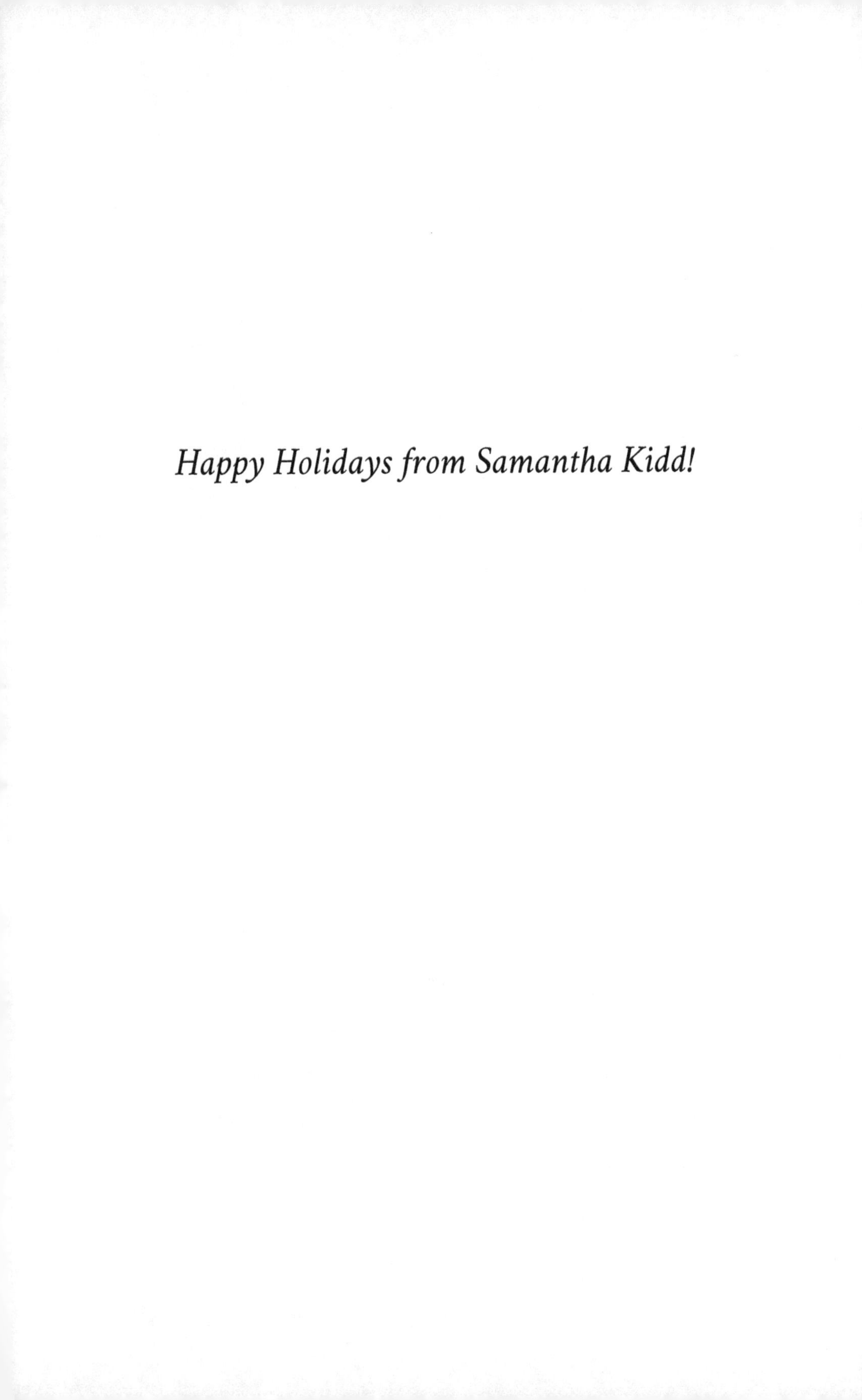

Happy Holidays from Samantha Kidd!

1

COZY NORTH POLE CHIC

For the first time in my life, I was wearing the wrong outfit. I could have let it ruin my night. I could have left the party and bought a new outfit. I could have hidden behind a Ficus in the corner.

"Relax, Samantha," Kyle said. "By this time tomorrow, everybody will have moved on to something new."

Kyle Trent was a former buyer like me, though we'd met through circumstances that had nothing to do with our work experience. His fiancé had been a murder victim a few years ago, and, as expected, he'd taken it hard. When the dust cleared, he quit his job at Tradava, the local department store where we'd met, and moved out of Ribbon, and I expected never to hear from him again, which was exactly how it had played out. Until last week when he called to find out if I had any interest in a temporary position for a publicity startup.

Being between employment gigs as I sometimes found myself, I said yes. Besides, free merch? Sign me up.

In the old days, before social media, what Kyle said would have been true. The days when you misread the dress code on a party invite and stand out for all the wrong reasons. But the old days were long gone, and this was my new reality. Even if the party attendees did forget about me when they left, by this time tomorrow the facial recognition feature on Facebook will have tagged me in the background of half a dozen posts, making my fashion faux pas live on indefinitely.

"How did this happen?" I asked Kyle. "The invitation said it was Cozy North Pole Chic."

Kyle stepped away and checked me out. "That's your version of Cozy North Pole chic?"

"Are we really going to pretend there is such a thing?"

The outfit in question was a red cable-knit sweater with red leggings and red suede knee-hi boots. I even wore a red Santa hat. I normally shied away from head to toe color, but it was Christmas, it was a party, and I've been told I look good in red.

Besides, it was cozy.

Just not as cozy as everybody else. To me, "cozy" meant "comfy." To them, "cozy" was the least important word on the invitation.

There were three women dressed in naughty Mrs. Claus outfits, at least four elves, and more sexy reindeer than I could shake a felt antler at. The men were in suits: red suits, green suits, red and white striped suits, snowflake-printed suits, and at least one Santa suit.

Santa and Mrs. Claus had been the subject of many photos.

Kyle wore a black velvet smoking jacket over a white T-shirt, black Adidas track pants with white stripes, and black leather high top sneakers.

He could have told me.

The job in question was a two-week freelance assignment with Brand Nue, a publicity firm that specialized in branding and social media campaigns. Kyle had first turned to our mutual friend Eddie Adams, who quickly said no. (I believe his exact words were, "Not on your life, dude.) (Actually, they were, "Not on your life, dude. You should ask Samantha Kidd. She's crazy enough to say yes.")

And I was. Even though my financial

situation has greatly improved in the past few years, I have a problem turning down jobs when they make themselves available to me.

We stood amongst the other employees of Brand Nue. There were the YouTubers who arrived with tripods and livestreamed the party from the corner, the Pinterest folks who scouted trends to add to their style boards, and Facebook people who huddled off to the side chatting with their friends online and letting people in other locations feel like they were part of the crowd.

And then there were those like Kyle: influencers paid to promote a lifestyle that people aspired to copy.

Kyle started working for Brand Nue two years ago and had built up a solid following. It didn't hurt that he could, if he wanted, turn in his influencer card for a job modeling for some All-American brand like J. Crew. But Kyle had learned how to craft posts that appealed to all sexes and all ages. He was equal parts bro and babe. If he could arrange to marry a Spice Girl, he'd give David Beckham a run for his money.

Fortunately for Kyle, I was happily married to the man of my dreams and had no interest in anything more than a working relationship. It was this that made us compatible influencers. Our entire friendship was fabricated for the online community, but the rest of the world didn't have to know that. All they knew was that Kyle was fabulous and I was fabulous and look at the fabulous events we often attended together.

Looking fabulous.

Two young women walked past. One was wearing a short white faux fur jacket over a cropped tank top, shredded jeans, and white pumps. The other was in an enormous white silk shirt with billowing sleeves over black leather leggings. Red shoulder-duster earrings and matching tassel necklace coordinated with her glitter-encrusted ankle boots.

"Hi, Kyle," the one in the fur said.

"Hi, Michelle," he said. "Nice coat."

She shrugged as if the choice of white faux fur worn slightly dropped over one shoulder was an afterthought. "Thanks." She glanced at me. No compliment followed. She looked back at Kyle, tipped her head and stuck out her thumb and pinky like a phone and mouthed, "call me," to him, and then turned around and walked away with her friend.

"How is that cozy?" I asked.

He laughed. He finished his eggnog and set the empty cup on a nearby tray. "Don't let this group get to you. The people in this room are more competitive than the cast of *Game of Thrones*. You have no idea what they'll do to look good."

"They look pretty good now. Or do you mean filters and Photoshop?"

"I mean followers and viral posts. These people are cutthroat when it comes to getting results." He elbowed me, and I followed his eyes to the young women who gave my outfit the cold shoulder.

They'd walked a few feet away from us. The one in the fur held up her phone and they pushed their heads together like they were taking a selfie. Only the phone was up in the air, aimed not at them, but at me.

The flash went off. The woman lowered her phone and they bent over the screen and giggled.

My inappropriate outfit would be a thing on Instagram within seconds.

"Okay, they're not so nice," I said. I checked the clock. "How long do I have to stay? I don't know how much more of this I can take."

"You need to relax. Go with the flow. This can't be the first time you stood out in a crowd."

"It's not, but in the past, I stood out in a good way."

"Tell you what. Kickin' It is dropping a

new sneaker at Pop Shop two nights from now. Did you get an invite?"

"No."

"You can be my plus one. Rumor has it they're scouting for someone to rep their line regularly, and I'd love that gig. Meet me in the morning and we can stage a couple of pictures early. When the party happens, you can pull the trigger on the photos and wipe out the memory of anything people post about you tonight."

"You don't mind?"

"I brought you into this, didn't I? I feel partially responsible."

"Then it's a deal. Tomorrow morning, outside Pop Shop, dressed for tomorrow night's launch party." I paused for a moment. "Just so we're on the same page, what were you thinking of wearing?"

2

TWELVE HOURS LATER

THIS TIME, THINGS WERE GOING TO BE different.

It had taken me far too long to get life to a point where I was happy—well, happy being relative, but—oh heck, I'll say it. I'm happy! It was a designation that, for longer than I care to acknowledge, seemed like I would never reach, but here I was. It was the kind of thought that makes you want to take stock of everything you have, everything that brought you to the moment where you're at, everything that you'd survived that led to being this happy, this satisfied, this willing to just stand still and smile and let the world know you have the perfect life. Like me. Samantha Kidd, living the perfect life.

At least that's what my new Instagram account, @xoSamantha, proclaimed in the bio field, and nobody ever misrepresents themselves on social media. Right?

"Dude, you look a little crazy," Eddie said.

Eddie was my sometime voice of reason and all times best friend. For the past twenty-some years he'd worked in the display department of Tradava. (Their demise had wreaked havoc on the lives of a whole bunch of people.) For the foreseeable future, Eddie had no plans greater raising money for a new skateboard park and enjoying his first non-retail Christmas since graduating art school two decades ago.

"I don't look crazy. I look happy."

"No, I'm pretty sure the look on your face says crazy."

I held my phone out in front of me and cocked my head to the side, set the timer to go off in five seconds, and pressed the shutter. While the timer counted down, I held my arm steady and tried to make sure both my head and the display of limited-edition sneakers were visible in the shot. I snapped a total of ten selfies and then dropped the ear-to-ear smile and scrolled through them.

Eddie was right.

I held the phone up again and snapped a few more photos. Eddie pulled the zipper on his black North Face jacket all the way up and shoved his balled-up fists into his pockets. His bleach blond hair, normally either shaggy or shorn into a mohawk, was hidden under a black knit cap.

From the get-go, I knew being an influencer was a temp job, and I had no interest in it being anything more. If not for the invitation that made its way to me via Eddie via Kyle, I wouldn't have sought it out.

But ever since Tradava closed, I had free time. And free time + too many pretzels = habits that were hard to break, and free time + free product = the perfect distraction. I'd had enough job struggles in recent years to know it was better to stay busy than not.

"I can't believe you took a job as an influencer. What does Saint Nick say about this?"

Saint Nick, a.k.a Nick Taylor, was my husband. Under his full name, he was a shoe designer, and under "Saint Nick" he was branching out into designer sneakers. The only thing he'd said about my new role as influencer was if it was something I wanted to do, I should do it.

"Nick's fine with this."

Eddie ignored my response. "If we weren't already friends, I'm pretty sure this," he pulled his hands out of his pockets and waved them around me and my phone, "would keep me from ever wanting to get to know you."

"It's because of you that I have this job."

"No, it's because of me the job was open. *I* turned it down like any sane person would."

"And you gave Kyle my name," I said. "I'm the same person I was yesterday, and the one I'll be tomorrow. Just a normal girl overdressed for a sneaker launch party. You love sneakers. You would see this post on Instagram and want to get to know me because you'd think I must be cool if I got an invite to this event."

"How? I wouldn't follow you because you look like a crazy person."

"You follow #sneakers, right? Or #sneakerbling or #slickkicks or #sneakerworld or—hold on." I pulled a sheet of paper out of my pocket and scanned the list of approved hashtags that had been emailed to me along with the coordinates for this event. "#sneakerlife, #sneakerdreams #sneakergoals—"

"Dude, it's seven in the morning, and

you're wearing gold lamé. Just because you're dressed for an event doesn't mean there is one. It's you and me and a cardboard backdrop." He flicked his fingers against the cardboard, and it wobbled. "Is this where the world is these days? People look at a picture on Instagram and think it's real?"

"It *is* real. We're standing here, aren't we? That's real. I'm dressed for the event, right? That's real." I pulled a photo of a QR code up on my phone. "I have an invite. That's real."

Eddie grabbed my phone. "The party doesn't start for another twelve hours and the backdrop to your pictures is printed on cardboard."

"That's how it works. My audience can't tell if the pictures were staged or not."

"Your audience? What audience? People who follow #crazyfashionchicks?" For the first time in the conversation, he cracked a smile.

"I resent that—well, I resent most of it. I'll

edit the rest of your hashtag and use #fashionchicks."

"It's so fake. Doesn't that bother you?" He waved his hands around, taking in the cardboard backdrop and then glanced down at my outfit. For a man who claimed to have cold hands, he did a lot of hand-waving.

"Whoa," I said. I threw my hands up in front of me and stepped back. "There is nothing fake about my outfit."

I spent two hours searching Pinterest for the appropriate but not overused representation of "urban glam street style."

Apparently, it was a thing.

Last night, I'd missed the mark so much I might as well have been Isaac Newton shooting arrows at dandelions instead of apples. Today, I left nothing to chance. I wore a short white boucle funnel neck sweater over a micro-pleated gold lamé midi-length skirt and white sneakers trimmed in gold leather. Oversized gold hoop earrings hung from my ears. My sleeves were pushed halfway up my forearms, exposing a (left) wrist of gold bangles, watch, and faux ruby cocktail ring. (When Eddie asked why I wore no jewelry on my right hand, I explained that it was the hand that held my phone. #Duh.)

"It's thirty-four degrees outside, and your sleeves are pushed up. You're not wearing gloves or a hat. How are you not freezing? If this were real, you'd be bundled up."

"It's not that cold," I said. A couple hurried past us. I would love to describe them to you, but their heads and faces were hidden behind wool hats, scarves, and bulky down coats that masked any identifying characteristics.

I was tired of Eddie being right.

"How many times do I have to tell you this job is about promotion?" I asked. "You worked in visual. You know product displays are what catch a customer's attention. That's what I'm doing. Posting about specific products through the depiction of an aspirational lifestyle in order to catch the public's attention."

"You can tell me as many times as you want. It won't make me see this as anything other than fake."

This wasn't the first time Eddie told me what he thought about the job he'd turned down, and truth be told, it was getting harder to ignore the very valid point.

Pretending to attend an exclusive sneaker launch before it took place and scheduling the post to appear on social media during a predetermined window of time given to me was the opposite of spontaneous. Yet if done correctly, my (and a whole bunch of other) posts would appear in the social media streams of anybody who followed the company-designated hashtags, and, if successful, get shoppers to drop everything to get in line for a pair of five hundred dollar sneakers of their own.

There were other people paid to stand in

line, making the general public feel like they were on to something hip, that they'd discovered an event that most of the world wouldn't learn about until it was over. When those people, the true target customers, posted pictures of the items they bought after leaving the event, they'd complete the third leg of the social media blitz by providing actual unpaid testimonials.

But I was getting ahead of myself. My role, the first part of the equation, was to show the world, through social media, the life they could live if only they shopped like I did. For the next two weeks, I was getting paid to be an influencer.

3

VIP

BEING A SUCCESSFUL SOCIAL MEDIA INFLUENCER involved a certain amount of subterfuge. Take my outfit, for example. Before the sun rose, I was dressed for an evening event. It was two degrees above freezing, but I wasn't wearing a coat. The image of the shop interior in question was printed on a portable backdrop and delivered to me as part of my assignment—sort of like the intel package an assassin gets when hired for a hit.

Actually, it's nothing like that. I would guess. The only knowledge I have of assassins and hitmen come from *Gross Point Blank* and Lawrence Block books.

Pop Shop, the pop-up store where events were held, was a storefront on Penn Avenue owned by the publicity company who, until December 26th, was my employer. By owning a space that could easily be outfitted for trends and temporary shopping venues, they were able to build a following and market a sense of urgency. If you liked sneakers and wanted the latest styles, then you had a forty-eight hour window to shop them. Two days later, the store could be selling fashionable doggie gear or ugly Christmas sweaters—or whatever a client hired Brand Nue to promote.

The way it worked was simple. Clients booked Brand Nue, who scheduled publicity parties to impact their business. One week before the party, a team from Brand Nue mocked up the store and photographed every angle. The photos were blown up and transferred onto portable cardboard backdrops that were distributed to influencers. It allowed us time to get the perfect shot and left us free to mix and mingle during the event. Clients wanted a party, not a room filled with people on their phones.

"Dude, can we eat already?" Eddie asked. He hopped from foot to foot. "I'm cold, and I'm cranky."

"Maybe black and white checkered Vans aren't the appropriate footwear for sub-forty-degree weather."

"I'm not taking appropriate clothing advice from you."

I glanced up and down the street. A recent snowfall had accumulated and melted, leaving behind wet, gray sludge on both the sidewalks and median. All of Ribbon was dingy, which made getting a good outdoor post for social media even more challenging. I'd considered setting an alarm to go off hourly during the night so I could check the photographic nature of the weather, but I was no longer a party of one, and that decision might have led to marital discourse. I'd only been married a little over a year and I didn't want to rock the boat just yet.

"Give me a second to make sure I can work with one of these pictures," I said. "I'm weaning myself from the filter that airbrushes my face because it feels phony."

"So there *is* a line you don't want to cross. Good to know."

I looked up from my phone and glared at him. "Can we dial back on the judgment? The last time I checked, I was getting a paycheck and you're not."

"And for the first time since I met you, you don't need the money."

Yes, there was that. It was true. When the new owners of Tradava sold the company instead of giving it new life, a sealed-envelope cash settlement had changed hands between them and the bank. Hundreds of people were given severance packages and interview opportunities for jobs nearby, including me.

I turned it all down for one reason. An anonymous donor made arrangements to pay me two hundred and fifty thousand dollars in a deferred tax annuity for my role in exposing the behind-the-scenes corruption that led to the company's troubles. It was my secret, shared with my husband Nick, my BFF Eddie, and my new financial manager, who recommended we invest the money and set up a trust that paid me interest quarterly. It was all very adult and responsible and, frankly, I was afraid to tell anybody else about it for fear it would turn out to be a dream.

"Give me a sec to find out if Kyle's on his way," I said. "When I talked to him last night, he said the company will pay a bonus if we coordinate our pictures. It makes it look more like we're at the actual event." I started a text but was interrupted when Eddie grabbed my phone and held it out of reach.

"Kyle's meeting you here?"

"Yes. Why? You guys are friends. What's the problem?"

"If I knew Kyle was coming, I would have pawned off your needs for a driver on him and stayed in bed."

"I went home after the party last night, but Kyle was just getting started. This was his idea, but if he pulled an all-nighter, then he might bail."

"Whose idea was it for you two to collaborate?"

"The company. I'm new and Kyle's not. They thought if we were seen together, it would give me a boost in followers. Plus, when two influencers are in the same shot, the client pays double our fee. Something about how it lends authenticity to the campaign."

"Your employer actually acknowledged that if two of you were in the same place, your photos might look more believable? I'm shocked. The next thing you know, they're going to tell you to show up on time and pretend you're at—wait for it—a launch party."

I shoved my phone into my pocket and gave Eddie my full attention. "The only thing people care about is how they look online. Ratings and viral posts, product placement and testimonials. Nobody advertises anymore. It's Instagram. And Facebook. And Pinterest and YouTube and Snapchat. It's this or nothing. You've got nothing. How's that working out for you?"

"I've got six months' salary in the bank and a fully vested 401K that I just rolled over into an interest-bearing mutual fund. I'm not worried."

A gust of wind blew around my ankles, reminding me that it was too cold to stand on a street corner, arguing the virtues (or lack thereof) of being hired to be a social media influencer for the holiday season. I scrolled through the photos to make sure one was useable and then sent Kyle a text:—*I'm at pop shop. you still coming?*—and waited for a response.

Brand Nue supplied us (all the influencers) with burner phones to use exclusively for the jobs. They were preloaded with filters, editing apps, and universal unlock codes. All contact information, communication, photos, and account details were considered proprietary. This allowed them to audit our activity and our whereabouts. If any unsanctioned leaks occurred, they could reverse-track the info to the location of the influencer and find out who was responsible. Not only was a leak grounds for immediate termination, but a penalty of ten thousand dollars came with it, which provided enough of a threat to keep us on the straight and narrow. (One would think, though the rumors surrounding my last-minute hiring suggested a violation had occurred, leaving Brand Nue in the lurch well into the holiday shopping season.)

While I waited for Kyle's response, Eddie rubbed his gloved hands together. "What are you waiting for?"

"I can't just up and leave. Kyle said he'd be here, and it wouldn't be professional to bail."

"Professional. Right."

When a reply didn't come, I sent two additional texts. I checked the settings on my phone to see if my location was visible (it was) and activated Find Me to send a ping to Kyle's burner. Eleven minutes and half a numb foot later, there was still no response.

"Dude, can't you just call him from your regular phone?"

"It's against company policy."

"Don't mention the company. Don't mention the job. Just tell him to check his burner and hang up."

"I suppose I can do that." I pulled my personal cell out of my pocket and glanced up and down the street to make sure I wasn't being watched. Despite the lack of people, I felt conspicuous. But Eddie was right. If I didn't mention work, there was nothing odd about me calling a friend on my personal phone. The only problem would be if it went to voicemail—

"Kyle?" answered a female voice.

I held the phone away from my head to make sure I'd hit the right contact. "Hi," I said tentatively. "I'm looking for Kyle Trent. Is he there?"

"No, he's not here. He's not anywhere. You know where he is? Because when I find him, he's a dead man."

4

NEW TERRITORY

"WHO IS THIS?" I ASKED.

"Candi. I'm his f***in' girlfriend."

"I'm Samantha Kidd. I'm—we're—I'm his colleague."

"You work for Brand Nue?"

"Yes."

She cursed again. It wasn't said with any maliciousness or venom, just a throwaway word the way I might have said "that's interesting" or "I see." I got the feeling Candi cursed a lot and that perhaps she used the F-word the way Eddie used "Dude." The difference was "dude" wouldn't get her a PG-13 rating, but her F-bomb would.

"That f***ing company has gone too far. Where's he at this morning? He must have been out all night. Or he's with Michelle. He thinks I don't know they met up two nights ago. If he thinks he can f*** around and expect me to be f***ing available, he's got another f***ing thing coming." She paused for a moment. "You sure he's not with you?"

"Why would I call his phone if he were with me? I haven't seen him since yesterday."

"At the denim store? Or that jewelry launch? There was a CD launch party in Lancaster. Were you there? F***ing music groupies. I knew I shouldn't have left him alone at that one."

How many parties had Kyle attended? "Candi, I'm married. Happily. Kyle and I are acquaintances at best. We were supposed to meet up this morning for a collab, but he didn't show."

"You call his f***ing burner?"

"I've been texting him for the past fifteen minutes."

"That f***er's phone is going to blow up by the time I'm done with him."

"Do me a favor?" I asked. "If you hear from him, will you tell him to call Samantha Kidd? I'm leaving Pop Shop so there's no point in him coming here."

"I'm not his f***in' answering service." She disconnected the call.

Despite watching Eddie hop around, I'd lost track of the temperature until now. Frigid air snaked under my skirt and up my legs. I wrapped my arms around myself and rubbed at my sleeves. It was close to freezing, and I was in urban glam cocktail attire. This was crazy.

"Let's get out of here," I said.

I packed up the cardboard backdrop while Eddie got his VW Bug and pulled around out front. I'd gotten a little too comfortable having

Eddie drive me around Ribbon, but since neither of us had any real place to go, it wasn't an inconvenience.

Financially, I was in new territory. The anonymous windfall came late enough in the year that, to defer taxes, my accountant suggested I not touch the money until January. The one exception was to charity. Donations were deductions, he'd explained, and the more I gave away, the less I'd give Uncle Sam. Being tasked to part with my money and not try to save for a rainy day (or spend on new clothes) was a whole different way of life.

The temporary job with Brand Nue came at the perfect time. It was enough money to enable my generous streak without guilt, but not so much that I'd be tempted to convert it to a full-time gig. You could make the argument that pretending to have everything in order to afford slightly more than nothing was a bit hypocritical, but then again, you could also argue that beggars can't be choosers.

A few minutes later, Eddie and I sat at a booth at Benedict's Eggs, a recently-opened breakfast spot in Ribbon. The waitress, a fresh-faced college-aged girl who used words like "Hon" and "Dear" came by to fill our coffee mugs. She wore a green and white Santa hat with beige elf ears stitched onto the side over straight brown hair, and a sweatshirt that spelled out "Ho Ho Ho" in gold sequins. Her nametag said, "Mabel." I made up a narrative about her: community theater going deep on research before auditioning for the part of Alice in a local production.

Either that or her quaint small-town act was affected to get her bigger tips.

"Aren't you cold, hon? It's close to freezing out there."

"I'll be fine." I rubbed my hands together and ignored the fact that my fingers were blue. “Bring the hottest pot of coffee just in case.”

“Give me one sec.” She went away and returned with steaming hot coffee that she poured before taking our order (cheese omelet for me, side of bacon, quinoa toast with avocado for Eddie).

When she was out of earshot, I recapped to Eddie what I’d learned when I called Kyle’s phone, which wasn’t all that much.

“She sounded upset. Not worried so much as angry. When she heard my voice, she immediately assumed Kyle was cheating on her with me, but after I assured her we were just colleagues, she said he was missing—had been for hours.”

I pulled my phone out and checked Kyle’s social media feeds. The last picture he posted had been last night during the party. It was arguable that he deserved eight hours to sleep, but Kyle was a master at keeping his page updated at minimum every four hours.

The frequency tripped the algorithms and kept his posts showing up to the most engaged of his fans. In short, he posted enough that people didn't have a chance to forget who he was.

The lack of updates troubled me.

"Do you know Candi? She said she was Kyle's girlfriend. She sounds like a real pistol."

"Kyle goes for that type," he said. "I don't know her, but I've met a couple of his other lady friends. They're all cut from the same cloth." Eddie rolled his eyes.

"What about you? Do you guys ever double date? Are you his wingman?"

"That's not my scene."

I would have given Eddie a hard time, but lately his "scene" involved driving around crazy fashion chicks—well, one in particular—and I didn't want to say anything that would rock the boat. Plus, I had yet to figure out the perfect gift for him, and the more time we spent together, the more likely I was to nail it.

"Did you guys ever hang together outside of work?"

"Sometimes. Not so much after he left Tradava, but he called when he heard about the store going out of business and we went to lunch. Fell right back into it like we'd been hanging out every day."

"Does him not showing up sound out of character to you?"

"I can't say. My friendship with Kyle was based on our working together. We saw each other all the time because we were both on a schedule. Has he ever bailed on you before?"

"No, but I've only been doing this for about a week. It could be he got tied up with something else. Candi said he had four parties yesterday, so maybe he crashed."

"Maybe he wanted a break didn't tell her where he was going."

"I could see wanting a break from her. She sounds a little rough around the edges."

I pulled my personal phone out and

checked the screen. No messages or calls. "If Kyle took another assignment, the publicist would know. Wait here." I stood up and walked to the restaurant lobby. It was a little after eight, too early to expect most businesses to be open, but I didn't know who else to call.

"Brandon Nue," answered a male voice.

The company was called Brand Nue, after the founder Brandon Nue. There was only one person who answered the phone using his name. Him.

Brandon Nue was a mixed-race millennial who'd defied the odds of being born to drug addict parents by parlaying his high school side hustle into capital that he multiplied with sound investments. Unlike other entrepreneurs born in his generation, he kept up his hustle through college. He opened Brand Nue Publicity upon graduation. Investors liked his enthusiasm and respected his drive. He could have worked for any number of them, but he wanted to work for himself.

It wasn't long before the publicity firm took off. Brandon eventually flexed his majority shareholder status and bought the company. He had no trouble getting or keeping clients. Enough of his market knew about Nue and signed on the dotted line, creating a demand for his magic touch.

"Brandon, this is Samantha Kidd. I started working for you last week?"

"Kyle Trent's referral. Right. What's up, Sam?"

"I prefer Samantha," I said. Brandon said nothing. "Have you heard from Kyle this morning? Or last night?"

"Sure. He called in for extra gigs, and I gave him a last-minute assignment. Why?"

"I tried to reach him this morning and he hasn't called back."

"On your burner?"

"Of course," I said.

I heard the sound of keys on a keyboard in the background, and then Brandon returned. "There's no cellular activity on your phone, just text."

He could see that? "That's right, I texted him. He didn't text back. We planned to coordinate a series of posts at Pop Shop."

"You said you called him."

"Figure of speech," I said quickly. "I meant I tried to get in touch with him."

"Too bad you weren't able to make that happen. Those pics would have been epic. Is there anything else?"

I hadn't expected the owner of the company to answer the phone, but he had, and I wasn't about to be rushed off. "I talked to his girlfriend this morning. She's was a little hysterical. She said she hasn't heard from him in hours."

"Who's this girlfriend?"

"Candi something."

Brandon laughed. "Hard Candi? Her

default setting is hysterical. Makes for some good stories, but not exactly a reliable source."

"I don't think you understand. Kyle's MIA. He hasn't answered my texts. He was a no-show at our meeting. His Instagram account hasn't had any activity for hours. I thought maybe you might know something?"

"Sam, Kyle's one of my best employees. He knows how to scout a backdrop and write a story. If I could clone him, I would."

"But you don't know where he is," I confirmed.

"I imagine he's in the field working on one of the last-minute assignments he just got," Brandon said. "When I hired him, he told me he'd do best if I gave him a long leash. I've never regretted that decision. He hit four parties yesterday, went to the annual office holiday party last night and the man knows how to party. It's not a big deal, Sam. Kyle probably just needed to crash for a few."

It wasn't the first time my active

imagination had jumped to conclusions and gone into overdrive. I'd already promised myself this morning that this time things would be different, and not even two hours after that vow, I'd failed. "Sorry to have bothered you."

"Hold up. Are you free today? A couple of assignments came in overnight. Last minute gigs. You can pick and choose, whichever accounts you feel like working. Payment in product. You said you were down with that. Can you come in to get collateral?"

"Sure," I said.

"Great. See you when you get here."

I returned to the booth and ate a piece of bacon. "Any luck?" Eddie asked.

"No. I talked to Brandon himself and told him what's what. He doesn't seem worried. He said Kyle probably just overslept."

"You sound like you don't believe him."

I shrugged. "I should. He's the boss. It's just that something doesn't . . . never mind."

Eddie leaned forward. "What?"

"I'm doing what I always do. This time things are going to be different." I picked up my phone and opened Instagram. "It's just . . . no."

"What is it?" Eddie asked again.

"I don't believe him," I finally said.

"How come?"

I found Kyle's account and scrolled through the posts. "What I'm being told and what I'm seeing don't fit. Brandon said Kyle is one of the best influencers in the business. And from everything I've seen, the reason he's so good is because he keeps up a steady stream of posts. If Kyle's that reliable, then why hasn't he posted anything for the past twelve hours?"

5

A NATURAL

EDDIE TOOK MY PHONE AND SCROLLED through the posts. "Dude. His whole life is on here. How can anybody live like this?"

"Kyle's a natural. He's good looking and appeals to men and women. He's got fifteen thousand followers including some pretty heavy hitters. People want to know how he lives, and he has no problem showing them."

"He's got a regulation-sized pool table and Coco Chanel's sofa. And did you see that shelf of crystal in the background? That's like forty grand of Daum. I had no idea he had that kind of money."

"He's got good taste."

Eddie dragged his finger up the screen and then back down. "And the whole world knows it. Doesn't he worry somebody's going to rob him?"

"That might not even be his house. Kyle's a master at staging his Instagram posts. That's why Brandon loves him. And that's why I was hired on Kyle's recommendation. I didn't even have to interview. I just signed some papers and picked up my welcome package."

"What was in it?"

The welcome package included a seven-hundred-page contract that I hadn't bothered reading. My temp assignment was to last two weeks, and it would have taken longer for me to read the contract!

"Some tips on how to create an engaging post. Hashtags, photo filters, stuff like that."

Mabel returned with our food. She set the plates down. “You need more bacon, hon?” she asked me.

“No, but I could use a top off on my coffee,” I said.

“Sure. How about you, sweetie?” Mabel asked Eddie.

“Yes, ma’am,” he said.

Mabel was at least fifteen years younger than us.

Eddie handed my phone back. “If all this worry is based on the hysteria of a woman with a jealous streak, you might want to take it with a grain of salt. Spend more time worrying about your own assignments and less about Kyle’s.”

I knew Eddie had a point, but it wasn’t enough to shake the feeling that something was wrong. Kyle’s vanishing act nagged at me all through my omelet, toast, bacon, and three coffee refills. I couldn’t let it go.

I paid the bill and tipped heavily to reward Mabel for her community theater and we left.

Eddie checked his watch. "Any more pretend social engagements, or are you done for the day?"

"I'm done. Why?"

"Good. I've got a meeting with the skateboard park committee. I'll drop you off on my way."

"Drop me at Brand Nue instead."

Brand Nue Publicity had an office on the eastern side of Penn Avenue across the street from the post office. The building was three stories, and the north east corner of all four floors was framed out in floor-to-ceiling windows that looked out over the street. The first floor was a bistro. The IT department was on two, and the main offices for Brand Nue were on the top. Eddie dropped me by the front entrance, and I went inside.

The bistro was filled with people. There appeared to be no one over the age of thirty (aside from me), and not for the first time I wondered about how millennials learned about hot new spots and decided which to frequent. Somehow, I'd missed the memo on traveling with a pack mentality.

A line stood to the left of the counter, and every person in the line was head down, looking at their phones. For people who liked to travel in groups, they didn't seem to converse much.

I bypassed the crowd, squeezed on an elevator with twenty other people, and flattened myself alongside the interior while most of them got off on the second floor. One man remained. He had dark hair worn short, a mustache, and a small beard trimmed into a point that left him looking devilish. He wore a neon green hoodie, camo pants, and Nike Air Force One sneakers in a color combination I was fairly certain wasn't available at the local Foot Locker. We rode in silence to the third floor. I hung back and adjusted the saggy crotch of the pantyhose I wore under my urban glam outfit while the man entered the Brand Nue lobby. My Instagram-worthy look was having its way with me and I couldn't wait to get home to change.

Brand Nue had been decorated in rusted-out-warehouse chic. The walls were exposed brick, the ceiling was exposed duct work, and the floor was exposed concrete. For all the fakery the influencers were expected to use in our posts, Brandon seemed to put a price tag on gritty reality.

To the right of the lobby was a semicircular desk that separated the receptionist from the seating area. The woman behind the desk was five feet tall with spiky white hair knotted in small clusters with colorful rubber bands, piercings through her eyebrows and nose, and a cropped sweatshirt that exposed the bottom half of her black bra. (Brandon's penchant for exposure may have been taken a bit literally by her.) She faced the man from the elevator with her desk between them. Despite the foot or so difference in their height, I sensed she wasn't intimidated. I wandered to the black leather sofa and sat down to wait until they were done. There was no point pretending not to eavesdrop; the lack of sound absorbing textiles combined with the size of the lobby made privacy impossible.

"I told you on the phone. Brandon doesn't want to talk about this." the receptionist said.

"He's been blowing me off for two days," the man said. "I ain't got time for this, ai-ight? Get the boss man on the phone and tell him I'm waiting for an assignment."

The man's voice was high, and if I'd heard it over the phone and not face to face, I would have wondered if I were speaking to a man or a woman. I gleaned from what he said that he was an influencer like me, and I took a more than causal interest in breaking down the individual parts of his look: his watch was Patek Philippe, his hoodie was Dsquared2, and his camo pants were G-Star. With minimal effort, steady hands, and a sharp pair of sewing scissors, he could have removed every tag on his outfit. It said more about him that he didn't.

"Take a seat or leave, your choice. Brandon is booked all day and there's no guarantee he can make time for you."

"This shizzle is in the ditch, yo."

A door opened behind the woman and Brandon Nue came out. Unlike the irate visitor, the publicist was simply dressed in a navy blue sweatshirt, plaid trousers, and white New Balance sneakers. His hair was shorn close to his head, and his face was clean shaven. His eyes, an unnatural shade of lilac, played against his dark skin and Asian features. He could have doubled as an extra in a Baz Luhrmann vampire movie, if such a thing existed.

"Are we okay out here, Rosha?" he asked. He put his hand on the chair behind the receptionist, not on her, but the gesture sent a silent message of who he supported in this power struggle.

"I was just telling Leon that your schedule was booked solid for today," Rosha said. "I gave him the offer of leaving or waiting in the lobby, and I believe he's weighing his options."

For the moment, the three people in the office appeared to not have taken notice of me. I sat with my hands folded in my lap and watched. (The only thing missing from the show was popcorn.)

"Brandon, yo, you gotta give me something. I haven't had an assignment since last week," Leon said.

"Since the Mackenzie party," Brandon said.

"Yeah, the Mackenzie party. That was a dope gig."

"Things got out of hand, Leon. The client expressed concerns after seeing your posts."

"That was an accident, man!" Leon said. He gestured with his hands, waving them up as if holding a giant watermelon.

"That picture from the bathroom cost you any future assignments from Brand Nue. We don't create content like that. If you'd read your contract, you'd know that. You have no business here. You can leave on your own or be escorted out of the building by security. As a parting gesture, I'll let you choose."

"It's the holidays, man. Cut me some slack. Last I looked, your books were overflowing with client needs. No way you hired somebody to fill my shoes already."

"Your assignments have been tasked out to another employee."

"Kyle Trent?" Leon said. "Dude's nothing but a wannabe. Can't fake it, can't make it. Everything he owns is on a thirty-day return cycle."

"Kyle follows the rules. You don't. It wasn't a hard decision to make."

Leon shook his head. "When the credit card companies catch up to your pretty boy, you're gonna lose your biggest so-called asset."

"With the money Kyle's making from your assignments, I think he'll be able to clear any debt he might have." Brandon kept his eyes on Leon but addressed his assistant. "Cut off Leon's access. Deactivate his phone and keycards. Archive his content on the cloud."

"You can't do that," Leon said.

"Goodbye, Leon," Brandon said. He moved out from behind the desk and put his hand on Leon's arm.

Leon jerked away. "I'm leaving, man." He stepped a few feet away. He pantomimed a gun with his index finger and thumb and aimed it at Brandon. "Cap," he said. He pointed at the receptionist. "Cap." He turned toward the door and seemed to notice me for the first time. He aimed at me. "Cap."

He opened his hands wide, fingers splayed, and held them up with his elbows bent. “A-B-See ya, wouldn’t want to be ya.” He stormed out of the office and pressed the button for the elevator. As the doors opened, he pulled a camouflage gun out of his waistband and tossed it on the floor.

6

ONE MARSHMALLOW SHORT OF A SMORE

I STOOD UP. "HE HAS A GUN," I SAID. PANIC rose in my chest. My voice quivered and I had to hold on to the back of the leather sofa for balance.

Brandon calmly left the office and picked the gun up from where Leon dropped it outside the elevator. He carried it inside. He fiddled with the muzzle and unwound a piece of matte tape that had been wound around it, revealing a bright orange plastic tip. He crumpled the tape in his fist.

"It's a toy?" I asked.

"It's a prop," he corrected. "We sent them out to our employees for the opening of a hunting store last year."

"That whole performance, the 'cap cap cap' thing, that means nothing? He's not unstable?"

Brandon smiled at me as though my assumption was charming. "Leon's theatrical. He makes people take notice. He was good influencer until his antics went too far."

"Was he right about Kyle picking up his assignments?" I asked.

Brandon nodded again. "Leon's success comes from shocking his followers. That behavior gets attention, but not always the right kind. We're having a higher success rate with family-targeted products and the clients don't want to pay someone like Leon who they can't control." He turned to Rosha and pointed to the gun. "Do something with that, okay?"

She picked it up and dropped it into the trash can next to her desk. "Done."

Brandon smiled at her and then looked at me again. His eyes narrowed slightly, and even though we'd just been taking, I got the feeling he was only now realizing he'd been talking to someone other than the usual office folks. He lifted his chin and nodded slowly, and then smiled at me. "Samantha Kidd. You're here for your next assignments."

"Yes. Mostly. I'm also here to talk to you about—"

"Follow me." He turned and walked through a door with no knob. It swung back, blending in with the wall.

"Go on, he won't bite," Rosha said with a wink.

I followed Brandon into his office. My legs were still feeling the effects of the adrenaline rush from when I saw the gun, but I didn't want Brandon to know that. I was unaccustomed to seeing a weapon and assuming it was fake. In my world, guns meant danger. I'd even been shot once. Eddie had mocked the phoniness of the influencer world and I'd defended it, but was this lack of fear the end result?

Brandon picked up a stack of shiny, colorful sealed bubble mailers and flipped through them. When he finished, he looked up at me. "Is your schedule clear?" he asked.

"Yes."

"Good." He handed me the stack. "Your posts aren't bad," he said, "but you need to loosen up a little. If you want to do well at this kind of work, you've got to find the truth in what you post. You have to believe it's real. You've got to sell it."

"I thought I was doing okay."

"Don't get me wrong—you're fine. A lot of my employees are fine. Fine's okay if that's all you got." He studied me and I gave him ample time to complete his assessment.

"I'm going to give you some advice." He lifted a remote from his desk and aimed it at the sixty-inch flatscreen mounted on the back wall. The screen filled with a series of Instagram feeds. He navigated to the third one on the left and clicked and there I was, filling all sixty inches. The photo was from the Ugly Christmas Sweater launch party, and there I was, surrounded by people dressed as reindeer. They looked like they were having the time of their life.

I looked like I was one marshmallow short of a smore.

"See that look on your face?" Brandon said.

I wish I didn't. "Yes."

"Good. That's you not letting go. That's you being aware that you're surrounded by people dressed as reindeer."

"How did you know what I was thinking?"

"It's written all over your face." He backed out of my Instagram feed and clicked on a different one. "See Leon? He was at the party for the final five minutes and he slayed. He blitzed his soc meeds with updates and his followers went nuts. The company reported a 37 percent increase after his posts went live."

"Thirty-seven percent is pretty amazing in a retail market," I said. In most retail circles, if a vendor could orchestrate a thirty-seven percent increase by paying someone to post about product, they'd do it in a heartbeat. "What happened?"

"He violated the terms of his contract. Grounds for immediate dismissal."

I waited, expecting Brandon to elaborate on what it was Leon had done. He didn't. I made a mental note to check Leon's Instagram account later.

As if reading my mind, he added, "The post has been deleted at the client's request," Brandon said. "Scrubbed from the internet. We wiped Leon's burner phone by remote access, too."

"You can do that?"

"Of course. Those phones belong to Brand Nue. So does the content."

"What if he took pictures with his personal phone?" I knew that also went against Brand Nue's policy, but judging from my first opinion about Leon, I didn't think he was much of a rule follower.

"If Leon shows any indication that he took pictures on a device that wasn't company-owned, he owes my company half a million dollars."

"Half a million?" I choked out.

"Yes. Standard terms. You read the contract, right?"

"Of course, I did," I lied. (Not only was it seven hundred pages long, there'd been a *Project Runway* marathon on that day.)

"Good." Brandon handed me the pile of colorful blister packs. "These jobs came in today. See what you can do with them. And try to loosen up, Sam. This isn't real life, it's only supposed to look that way."

I carried my new stack of assignments out of the office. Rosha had left a sign taped to her monitor—*in restroom*—so I left without saying goodbye.

I headed down to the bistro. Before calling for a taxi, I stood in line behind a squad of young women dressed in complimentary shades of pink. Slowly, the line advanced. A group of men, probably also of recent-college-graduation age, stood off to the side, oblivious to their surroundings, texting with one hand and holding coffee cups with the other. Normal coffee shop activity buzzed around me. I relaxed. It was just another day in Ribbon. This was a corporate culture, these people had jobs, and life would go on.

I carried my coffee to an empty seat by a heater and texted Kyle again. *Sorry I missed you this morning. New assignments from Brand Nue. Want to coordinate posts? LMK.*

I set the phone down and waited for a response. None came. Last night this was his idea, but today it was like that conversation never happened. That was weird, right?

Maybe. Maybe not. Maybe I was telling myself what I needed to believe.

A few months ago, I made the acquaintance of a life coach who taught me we sometimes make up stories that we believe that shape the way we interact with the world. She said if I believed I couldn't hold a steady job, I'd always have trouble finding a steady job, and if I believed Nick would get tired of me, then Nick would get tired of me. She said I needed to recognize my limiting behaviors and rewrite my stories.

At the first sign of trouble, I had a habit of jumping to conclusions. Sometimes I was right to do so, and other times, my conclusion-jumping put me in hot water. This thing with Kyle was a perfect example. When he didn't show and didn't take my calls or texts, I jumped to conclusions and assumed the worst.

So what if a jealous ex-girlfriend answered his phone and accused me of—something?

Brandon said hysteria was Candi's default setting. For all I knew, she was a stalker who invented a relationship with a public figure and factored me into her made-up narrative.

Maybe Kyle was burned out. Or tired. Or avoiding a needy, stalkery woman.

The truth was, I didn't know much about Kyle's personal life. I didn't know much about him at all, except that he'd lost the love of his life a few years ago. That kind of thing has to affect a person. I just didn't know how it had affected him.

Plus, Leon had said something about Kyle's debt, and even Eddie, who was friends with Kyle, was surprised by how Kyle lived. This lifestyle attracted people who liked the high life. The pressure to look successful trumped everything, and it was possible Kyle had overextended himself in his desire to build a brand. Short of hacking into his banking account to check the balance of his credit cards or his FICO score, I didn't know how I'd find that out. And since my only experience with hacking was that bronchial infection I had last year, I was staring down a dead end.

As I sat at the table drinking my coffee, I studied the other patrons in the bistro. Who were these people? What did they do here?

It was no wonder a company like Brand Nue succeeded. Every person in the room was on their phone. Sales campaigns weren't launched in print magazines and billboards anymore. They were two-inch square images on social media that pretended to illustrate seemingly normal people living the life you wanted to live.

It was a foreign concept to me, someone who'd grown up learning about style from the local shopping mall, but to the new world, if it didn't show up on Insta, it wasn't worth knowing about. And if you were the first one to spot a hot trend and adopt it yourself, you had cred. That's what made successful influencers so valuable. We could leak out information in a way that a company could not. Our role took the sleazy sales aspect out of selling.

I dismissed the memory of Eddie's words: *it's so fake. Doesn't that bother you?*

Being in my own version of Rome, I cued up Instagram and searched my feed for trends. I scrolled through cat videos, pictures of the Eiffel Tower, and a couple of inspirational quotes from Buddha.

What I still didn't see was a post from Kyle.

I hadn't posted for a few hours and the key to keeping you audience engaged was posting with some degree of regularity. I pulled a rose gold pen out of my handbag and laid it next to a glitter-encrusted notebook, staged my coffee to the right of it, and snapped. I added a catchy comment about powering up for a big day, added a couple of hashtags, and clicked Post. It was after the post went live that I noticed a new Instagram Story by Kyle Trent at the top of my screen.

Instagram Stories were ephemeral posts that vanished after twenty-four hours. They could be live, video, a series of images, or a picture with a caption. They showed up at the top of the page and sometimes throughout, if the good folks at Instagram decided you didn't mean to ignore them the first time. I liked knowing my posts would be there when I needed them, so at the onset of my temporary job as an influencer, I chose not to bother learning that feature.

Apparently, Kyle did not share my opinion, because there it was. A post by @TheRealKyleTrent.

I clicked.

It was a fuzzy image, poorly lit and out of focus. I magnified the shot, trying to see what he was promoting. Writing appeared, letter by letter, over the top of the dark image. The effect would have been mesmerizing if not for the six-letter message that the letters spelled out: *Help Me.*

For the past few hours, my gut feeling about Kyle had been explained away by multiple people. Even I'd started to think I was wrong. But no pat reasoning explained this.

It was no longer about Kyle needing to crash or not returning my calls or avoiding a jealous woman who claimed they were dating. This message came directly from the source, and that scared me more than anything.

7

JUST RIGHT

I STARED AT THE SCREEN, UNABLE TO LOOK away. Was this what I thought it was? Was Kyle legitimately using a social media account to send a message for help? Or was this part of a campaign to which I hadn't been assigned?

The top of the image said 8H. The story was eight hours old. Kyle had posted it after midnight last night. The time stamp also told me if Kyle didn't add anything to the story, it would go away at the twenty-four-hour mark.

If Kyle were really in trouble, I had sixteen hours to help him.

The stack of assignments sat on the vacant seat next to me. It stood to reason that Kyle would receive the same assignments that I did, especially since I was his referral. I tore the top package open and pulled out the contents. It was an invitation to a tasting at the whiskey bar on Penn Avenue. I'd spent a fair amount of time there recently while a colleague—oh heck, a homicide detective who didn't return my calls—recovered from a shooting in the hospital, and I'd learned it was a cop bar.

Too uncomfortable.

I set the invitation to the right of me and tore into the next envelope. Instructions and coordinates for a shopping party in Lititz.

Too far.

The third envelope contained details for a travel agency promoting trips to Florida. A password protected site (plus password) promised downloadable backdrops that we were encouraged to use to make it appear we were enjoying holiday fun in the sun.

Too phony.

The last envelope looked familiar. I pulled the tab to reveal the contents and found details about the launch party for Kickin' It, the sneaker company promoting a new product drop. The company was a repeat client with Brand Nue, and they were one of Kyle's favorite accounts. Of all the accounts we had, it was that one he was the most interested in because of the potential for future gigs.

Just Right.

Christmas sweaters and holiday parties were seasonal. They were jobs that came in during the latter half of December and dried up come the new year. But sneaker drops were big business. If Kyle could get himself established in that world, he'd have steady money coming in year-round.

Along with a fresh supply of the most coveted sneakers on the market, which may not mean a lot to a fashionista married to a shoe designer, but to someone like Kyle it could be huge.

Kyle hadn't shown this morning, and we'd set that meeting up last night. Before he posted the IG story. What had happened since then? Where had he gone, and what had he done?

"Hey, Sam. I thought you'd be gone by now." I looked up and saw Rosha hovering next to me. Her cropped top left her bare stomach inches from my head. Her pants, mostly utilitarian except for the low rise, were belted tight across her hips, leaving the curve of a muffin top just above the waistband. I'd spent years wearing undergarments intended to smooth out any bulges under my clothes, and I found it oddly empowering to see her proudly displaying the reality of her body.

She held a tray with a vanilla cupcake with white icing and green sprinkles and a green juice that matched her eyes. "The restroom on three has been out of order for two days. You know what's counterproductive? I come down here to pee and buy a green juice when I'm done. Never ending cycle. Can I join you?"

I swept the pile of opened blister packs from the seat to my tote bag. "Sure."

She sat her tray down first and then lowered herself onto the chair. "Sheesh! It's cold down here."

I glanced at her crop top. "I thought it was me."

"No, it's definitely not you. It's this building. The architect cared more about how it looked than how it functioned, and none of the tenants want to take on the cost of insulating those double-paned windows. When we moved into the building, it was so cold we could see our breath."

"How do you get anything done?"

She tipped to the side and lowered her voice. "I keep a portable space heater by my feet." She sat up. "I heard about your outfit at the holiday party. Sorry I missed it. I love when people go ironic."

Ironic? I'd take it.

"Were you there? I didn't see you."

"Nope. I had a family thing in Jersey. I took a long weekend and chillaxed with my sisters. I love my family, but by the fourth day, I couldn't wait to leave."

She tipped her cupcake and tapped it against the lining of her tray. Half of the sprinkles fell off. She slowly peeled the paper and then bit half. She chewed a few times, swallowed a gulp, and took another bite. It was as good a demonstration of wanting what someone else had as the best Instagram post and I regretted not getting a cupcake too.

"How come you're still here?" she asked. "I would have thought Neon Leon's stunt had you running out the front door."

"Neon Leon?"

"The guy with the gun. That's his profile name. He's always in neon. Sometimes it's orange, sometimes it's green. One time it was tie-dye. Looked like rainbow sherbet."

"Did you tell him that?"

"I did." She laughed. "He hasn't worn it since. Some influencer."

Five minutes ago, I'd been ready to dash out of the building and search for Kyle under every photographable backdrop in Ribbon, but the presence of Rosha offered a different idea.

How to best broach the subject? "I got the feeling Leon and Kyle don't get along."

"They used to be friends, but the rivalry took over. After Leon's stunt, Brandon pulled him from the rest of his assignments and gave them to Kyle. Leon flipped. Those two battle it out for top post daily, but that put Leon over the edge."

"Is that why he showed up with that prop gun? You didn't even break a sweat when he pulled it out, but to someone like me, that's a threat."

She laughed. "Nobody was going to see that gun but me and Brandon. Leon knew we would know it's a prop. Did you notice how he was dressed? Neon hoodie and camo pants that matched the gun? That's classic Leon. He does something crazy, and then he stages a shot that only Brandon can access from one of the cameras in the lobby."

"There are cameras in your lobby?" I felt a flush of heat climb my face as I remembered my apparently-not-so-subversive adjustment of my undergarments before entering Brand Nue's lobby.

"Sure. It's in the contract. You read it, right?"

That contract again! What else did they bury in that rival to *War and Peace*?

"Um, sure. What were you saying?"

"Leon isn't as dumb as he seems. He only comes to the office in person when he has something to stage. Today, it was that image while he was waiting for the elevators.

Perfectly framed. Brandon's upstairs with the legal team trying to figure out if they can use the image without Leon's permission since he was on company property."

"Can he?"

"Legal said no. Leon was outside the doors by the elevator wells. That's considered common ground and not proprietary to Brand Nue."

"I thought Brand Nue was in charge of distributing assignments to influencers?"

"They are. But if Brandon can get a shot to sell, he will. Publicity is the name of the game and money drives that car. Influencers can only do so much. A boost from something like this, some caught-on-security-camera image that makes the news can work wonders for all parties involved. Even better, because he doesn't pay endorsement fees for those shots."

"Wouldn't Leon rather take jobs that pay? If he was upset about Kyle getting his assignments, then why would he want to give away the goods for free?"

"A photo like that will give Leon a big boost in visibility. Once the image is leaked, people go to work exposing who he is. That leads to followers, which leads to more lucrative assignments. The company who provided the product isn't going to shy away from the spotlight either. Depending on how viral a story goes, they could sign him to a contract, or make a statement denouncing his activities, or anything, really, to keep the story in the front of readers."

Wow. I'd thought a staged Instagram post was fake but inciting an incident in the lobby of a public building all to get a picture for the 'gram took things to a whole other level. I had no idea what kind of world I entered when I took this job.

I guess I should have read that contract.

I had a zillion questions for Rosha, starting with the moral compass of

Brandon Nue—something I hadn't even considered before this conversation—and ending with the assignments that had been redirected from Leon to Kyle. Our conversation was cut short by an insistent buzz of her phone.

Rosha glanced at her screen. "That's as long of a break as I've ever gotten," she said. She stood up and sucked in her tummy. "Time to earn my paycheck."

I'd been toying with the idea of asking Rosha what she thought about Kyle's disappearance, but her willingness to talk about Brandon had raised a whole other set of questions. There was no doubt where her loyalty lay at Brand Nue—with her boss. But still, she saw things and knew things and maybe she could help.

I put my hand on her wrist to keep her from turning away. Her diamond-inlaid watch was cold to my touch, but the skin of her wrist was hot. She glanced at my hand and I immediately let go. "Rosha, when's the last time you heard from Kyle?"

"Sam, don't you worry about Kyle. There's a boatload of money headed his way thanks to Leon's poor judgment. Kyle can't walk away from a paycheck like that." She pointed at the stack of assignments in my tote. "You'd be better off if you started planning out your next post. Brandon had me check your feeds before I came down here and aside from that coffee cup shot, you haven't posted a thing for almost twelve hours. It's almost like you don't even work here. Keep it up and you won't."

8

CHEAP PASSENGER

ROSHA HAD A VALID POINT: I WAS NEGLECTING my job. I was less concerned by the loss of income than I was the loss of contact to Kyle. If he were in trouble—and his Instagram Story indicated he was—then I needed every lead possible to help him.

But first, I had to get organized.

And to get organized, I had to get home. Eddie would be tied up at the skateboard park for the foreseeable future, so I called Mo, my favorite taxicab driver. He'd moved to the states with the goal of becoming a taxi driver (not because of Robert De Niro) as a means of support for him and his sister. His professionalism had helped me out of a scrape a few years back, and I kept him on speed dial ever since.

"Miss Samantha! I am on my way home from the airport. Siri says I will arrive to you in eleven minutes."

"Great. I'll be waiting."

"But it will take me much longer than Siri thinks. I do not drive over the speed limit."

"I know, Mo. It's cool. I'll be fine."

"If you are cool, then go inside where it is warm. Then you will be fine. I will see you soon."

"I am inside. I meant—never mind. See you soon, Mo."

MINUTES LATER, I slid into the backseat of Mo's cab with my bulging handbag, a large coffee, and a cupcake. (#NoWillpower.)

"Miss Samantha!" Mo beamed. "It has been a very long time since you have called me for a drive." He reached behind my seat and handed me a small bottle of water. "I am competing with the Uber company these days. I have found my way to stand out."

I held up my coffee cup. "Save the water for another passenger. I've got coffee."

"You are a cheap passenger," Mo said. "I am happy to save the money for you."

I'd met Mo a few years ago when I found myself living out of a hotel room. Having a taxi driver on speed dial turned out to be helpful, especially after my car was destroyed. Mo's sunny disposition and charming grasp of the English language kept him popular amongst Ribbon residents who needed rides to the airport or sometimes into New York City. Uber had impacted the financial solvency of cabbies the country over, but Mo had come out relatively unaffected by the competition. I sometimes daydreamed about buying him a sleek sedan and hiring him as my driver, but I was savvy enough to know that my dream wasn't his and kept my daydream to myself.

"Am I taking you home, Miss Samantha?"

"Actually . . ." I let my voice trail off. There was one person I could talk to about the Kyle situation. One person who had nothing to do with the fashion industry or the influencer industry. Former homicide detective Loncar, who knew about something else: the investigation industry. "Take me to Kenhorst Plaza," I said. "I don't know the address, but I'll recognize the building when I see it."

Mo asked if I minded if he played his language lessons while we drove (I did not). I rested against the seat while he repeated phrases after a gentle female voice.

"It occurred to me that I forgot your birthday," the female voice said.

"It occurred to me that I forgot your birthday," Mo repeated.

"It occurred to me that we belong to the same gym," the female voice said.

"It occurred to me that we belong to the same gym," Mo repeated.

"It occurred to me that the price of homes are more expensive here," the female voice said.

"It occurred to me that the price of homes are more expensive here," he repeated.

"Is more expensive," I interjected.

"I do not understand," Mo said. He paused the lesson.

"The price of homes *is* more expensive, not *are* more expensive."

"But the lady says the price of homes are more expensive."

"She is wrong."

"She cannot be wrong. She is my teacher."

"Sometimes teachers are wrong, Mo."

He was quiet for a few seconds. "It

occurred to me that figuring out the English is more difficult than I expected."

"Most things worth figuring out are."

About ten minutes and two and a half lessons later, Mo pulled into a strip mall parking lot. I scanned the storefronts until I found the one I wanted. *Loncar Investigations* was printed on a sign that sat in the window between cheap horizontal blinds and a double-paned window. Aside from a couple of unreturned phone calls, I hadn't had any contact with Loncar since he left the police force. A part of me wondered if there really was a person on the other side of that door.

I handed Mo a twenty to cover the fare and tip. "Can you wait here?" I asked. "Keep the meter running," I added quickly. "I don't know how long I'll be."

"If I am to keep the meter running, then why are you offering me money now?"

"It occurred to me that you might like something to eat."

He took the bill. "You are very astute, Miss Samantha."

While Mo headed to the coffee shop in the corner of the strip mall, I went directly to Loncar Investigations. The door was open. Inside, Geri Loncar, the detective's daughter who I'd met recently while planning his retirement party, sat behind a white modular desk that could have come from Ikea.

"Samantha!" she cried. She jumped up from her chair and ran around the desk to hug me.

Geri was a recent mother who hadn't concerned herself with the pregnancy pounds she'd gained. Her red hair was pulled back in a low ponytail. She wore a Black Watch plaid sweater over Black Watch plaid pants and Black Watch plaid shoes. The exact same outfit was on a mannequin at Talbots. Apparently the 3rd Battalion Royal Regiment of Scotland was having a moment this year.

"Hi," I said. "You work for your dad?" I

lowered my voice. "How's that working out?"

She rolled her eyes. "I'm only here until he finds a real employee. Honestly, I needed to get out of the house. I've spent the last two years knitting baby scarves for my Etsy shop. You know what nobody tells you about going into business for yourself? There's nobody to talk to but yourself."

"Do you get a lot of good conversation here?"

She smiled. "At least here, I get dental."

Geri moved back to her desk and glanced down at her calendar. "Is he expecting you? I don't see an appointment."

"Something came up, and I was hoping he could see me without one." What I didn't say was I doubted he'd see me if I'd called in advance.

"Samantha Kidd."

Geri and I turned toward the man who stood in the doorway. He was in his sixties with thinning hair and a clean-shaven face.

He'd lost weight since the last time I saw him, probably in part due to his retirement and cut-off supply of donuts.

"Hi, Detective," I said.

He turned away from us and walked back into his office. "Come on back, Ms. Kidd."

I watched Geri. She pointed the end of her pencil at the door. "You better get back there before he changes his mind."

"Thanks."

I went into Loncar's office and closed the door behind me. It looked as though a decorator had watched *The Maltese Falcon* and used it as a template. Beat-up wooden desk filled with papers, stacks of paper, and secondhand sofa of questionable origin. A bottle of whiskey sat on the corner of his desk. I picked it up and discovered it was filled with unpopped popcorn kernels. (My kind of whiskey.)

Loncar sat in the chair behind the desk, leaving me to either stand or sit in the sofa of questionable origin. “Ms. Kidd. To what do I owe the pleasure?” he asked.

“That’s it? After all we’ve been through? No ‘how’ve you been,’ no ‘nice to see you’?”

“I’m no longer on the payroll of the Ribbon police force. My income is not derived from taxpayer money, and I’m not beholden to standards written by a mayor I had no say in electing.”

I wasn’t such a fan of the mayor myself, but that was a different issue.

“I have a case—I mean, I have a problem. And that problem comes with questions that are of the sort you’re versed in and I’m not.”

“Is this a matter for the police? Because, as I said, I am no longer a member of the police force.”

I dropped onto the sofa. It was more comfortable than I expected, and I sank deep into the cushions. “One of my colleagues is missing,” I said. “It’s been less than twenty-four hours, and I don’t know enough about his personal life to say if there are family members who would notice in time to notify official channels."

Loncar stared at me. This was new territory for us. In the past, I got involved in one of his cases, he told me to stay out of it, and I ignored him. We often ended up figuring things out around the same time, usually me with enough of a lead to put me in life-threatening danger and him batting clean-up.

We were kind of like partners.

"I should mention I'm still happily married. This is a colleague at a job that is a temporary holiday position for me but appears to be his ongoing line of work."

Loncar drummed his fingertips against the desk.

"I should also mention I have access to his network, but so do a lot of people, so that may not be the safest way to start our investigation."

Loncar coughed.

"One more thing. I have money. I'm not asking for a favor. I don't want you to do your job for free. If you'll listen to what I know and advise me on how to proceed, I'll pay you for your time."

Loncar sat still.

"Nice office," I said. I patted my hand against the arm of the sofa. "This sofa, though, doesn't say success. It kind of says 'if you're homeless, you can sleep here.' People probably sit in it and don't want to leave. You would do a lot better with something a little less inviting, you know, keep the riff raff from overextending their welcome. A little extra income could take care if that, if you catch my drift." I winked.

"Ms. Kidd, so we're clear. Are you offering to buy me a new sofa in exchange for advice on an unconfirmed missing person situation?"

"Would that be so wrong?"

9

PUBLICITY STUNT

LONCAR PULLED A YELLOW LINED LEGAL PAD and a ballpoint pen out of his desk drawer. "Let's start with some facts. Who's missing?"

"Kyle Trent. You might remember him from—"

"The murder at Heist. I remember. What's the job?"

"Social media influencer."

Loncar didn't move, but I saw him pause for a moment before writing it down. "When's the last time you saw him?"

"Hold up," I said. "You don't want to know what a social media influencer is?"

"I know what a social media influencer is."

"Great. Then you probably know all about hashtags and product placement and viral posts, right? And algorithms and Instagram stories and—"

Loncar sat back in his chair and set down his pen. "Let's start with Mr. Trent's last twenty-four hours. When did you first learn he was missing?"

I walked Loncar through what I knew. "Kyle and I were at a party last night. I left early. We were supposed to meet up this morning for a couple of photos to use later today, but he didn't show. When I tried to track him down, I found out he never went home. Nobody has heard from him since."

"That's it?"

"No, that's not it. He posted an Instagram story that said 'Help Me.'" I pulled my phone out and cued up the screen. Two hours had passed since the last time I watched the story. I was down to fourteen hours before it vanished for good.

I handed the phone to Loncar and he watched the brief video. A few seconds later, his face turned pink. He handed the phone back to me and I saw that the story following Kyle's had come from my favorite lingerie company and Loncar had gotten an eyeful of a curvy model in her bra and panties.

"I can't tell you anything about that Instagram story except it looks like a cry for help," I said.

"Or a publicity stunt."

"I don't think so."

Loncar's first thought had been nagging at me since the second time I watched the story. It played into what Kyle had told me the night of the office Christmas party. Something about influencers being competitive and how far they'd go for attention.

I spent the first day in the field with Kyle.

It could have been awkward, but it wasn't. We fell into a comfortable shorthand of similar tastes, knowledge of designers, and retail buying history to get along without the added inconvenience of romance. Kyle and I knew enough details about our respective personal lives to avoid the conversation completely. And with Eddie preoccupied with fundraising for the local skateboard park and Nick working on Saint Nick (the name was both a representation of good will and a nod to the nickname he'd picked up for being married to me), I was happy to ride shotgun with a public figure.

Loncar's suspicion played into how I felt when I completed my first assignment. I posted a picture and used the designated hashtags. For a few seconds, I felt anxious and sick.

When I worked for a luxury retailer in New York City, my credibility in fashion was sanctioned by their name on my business cards. Years (and a string of jobs) later, I was flying solo. I was a nobody in a sea of people who'd been testing products, appropriating trends, and perfecting selfies for the past five years. Would anybody care what a former fashion buyer said about a new product?

Before sixty seconds passed on my post, it had four hundred loves.

The followers came next.

It was like a dopamine hit. The immediate response from strangers who commented with emojis of adoration created feelings of happiness, pleasure, and satisfaction, all from a picture with a carefully crafted caption.

I remember turning to Kyle. "Did you see that? Four hundred loves in the minute after making my first post. People are going nuts. I might have a natural talent for this."

It was then that Kyle gave me the advice that stayed with me to this day. "Those initial loves come from Brandon's Instagram farm on the second floor. They're paid to monitor

Brand Nue accounts and trip the algorithms. I'm not saying you won't be good, but you were never going to fail. Brandon won't let you."

"Brandon keeps a staff of people whose job it is to like our posts?"

He nodded.

"Then these posts are rigged. Why bother trying to make them look authentic?"

Kyle tapped my phone. "Your name is on there. Your image. It's your choice if you want to stand for something and inspire people or if you want to be a two-dimensional puppet available to the highest bidder."

From that point on, I'd watched Kyle do the job and followed his lead.

I brought my attention back to Loncar. "Look at Kyle's social media feeds. He doesn't just post product. He posts motivational stuff and some shots that don't even include him. And selfies from his private life. There's no compensation for that. He doesn't do that for fame or money. He loves having a platform to inspire people. He does it so he can stand for something."

"I know a lot of people who love what they do and game the system at the same time."

"Do you? Really?" I watched Loncar and waited for his response.

The question appeared to take him by surprise. He didn't answer right away, which I took as indication that he wanted me to keep talking. (In the past, he shut me up with threats of arrest, and don't think my behavior wasn't informed by the fact that said threat was off the table.)

"You know corrupt cops. You know people affiliated with the mafia. You know criminals. You know a lot of people who wanted to get away with something, not because they loved what they were doing, but because they felt some sense of entitlement or greed. Those people you arrested were guilty. Ask yourself how many of them were happy doing what they were doing? How many of them loved their lives and committed those crimes anyway?"

"Good point. Continue."

I smiled. He didn't. I got serious and kept going. "When Kyle didn't meet up with me this morning, I texted him, but he didn't answer."

"Where's this phone now?"

Crap. My burner was in my handbag. Social media and technology were making it difficult to operate off the grid. I pulled it out of my handbag and set it on Loncar's desk. "Keep talking."

"I called Kyle's personal cell and a woman answered. She wanted to know who I was and where was Kyle. She said she was his girlfriend and she hadn't heard from him long enough to worry."

"What's her name?"

"Candi. She goes by Hard Candi on Instagram." Loncar didn't write it down.

"These people exist in the world of online IDs, not names. I'm sure you can find her full name if you do a little digging."

"Pink hair, swears like a sailor?"

"The cursing part is right. I don't know what she looks like. We've only spoken on the phone. Why?"

"Hard Candi, a.k.a. Candi Konopelski is no stranger to the law. She's a repeat offender who's been in and out of the system since she turned eighteen."

10

BANK

"What did Candi do?" I asked.

"Misdemeanors. Petty theft, robbery. Check fraud. She tried a couple of cons that backfired on her. Haven't heard her name in a couple of years. Started to wonder if she straightened up for good or moved on to new territory."

"Would she have to disclose those crimes on a job application?"

"Felony, yes. Misdemeanor, no. She's been smart enough to keep her crimes on the conservative end of things." Loncar sat back and pushed the papers away from him. "How much money do you make at this influencer thing?" Loncar asked.

"Excuse me?"

"You said it was temporary. It's not your life's work. I want to know where the money is in this thing, because if Candi's playing a con, she's going after the money."

"The money isn't with me. Half of my assignments pay out in free merchandise and the other half pay a flat fee of fifty dollars per assignment."

"For all influencers or just temps?"

"In this world, I'm a nobody. The equivalent of a Christmas hire at a department store. Brand Nue Publicity hired a bunch of people to help promote local businesses in the rush up to Christmas. Most of the temps are just doing it to offset the cost of their Christmas shopping. Brand Nue loves me because when I'm given the choice, I take payment in product."

"You get anything good?"

"Not yet. If Candi is after money, then she's after Brandon Nue. He owns the publicity firm that booked us all and between the incoming client funds and the money he makes from investors and other jobs year-round, that man has bank."

Loncar wrote *Hard Candi* and *Brandon Nue* on his legal pad. "Any other names I should know?"

"Neon Leon. Beefed up muscleman who only wears neon. He seems like a loose cannon. Apparently, he was fired, and Kyle got his assignments."

"When you say assignment, what do you mean?"

"Product endorsements. These guys are established influencers. For them, maintaining a way of life and telling their followers about it is big money."

"How much?"

"I don't know. A lot more than I make, if I had to guess."

Loncar wrote "Neon Leon" on his legal pad. "You got a last name for Leon?"

"No, but you can get it from Brand Nue."

Loncar set his pen down. "If I want to talk to this Brandon Nue, is he going to cooperate?"

"Talk to Rosha. She's the office manager and knows everything. But don't trust everything she says. She's one of them." I paused. I tried to picture Loncar walking into Brand Nue and asking for information. I'd had an easier time picturing the waitress from Benedict's Eggs as the lead in community theater. "These people speak a language you . . . might not know. How are you going to represent yourself?"

"What do you mean?"

"You can't flash your badge because you don't have a badge. And according to everybody I've asked, this is just Kyle taking a breather from public life. If he really is in danger and any of these people are responsible, you showing up and looking under rocks is going to freak them out. We'll lose every lead we have. But if we had someone on the inside, we could get access."

"I thought you were on the inside."

"I'm a holiday temp. I'm on the fringe at best. I could try to break into Brandon's office and go through his files—" It wasn't the best idea I'd had, but it was the only one I came up with on short notice.

Loncar cut me off. "Let's hope it doesn't come to that." He leaned forward and tapped the end of his pen on my phone. "Show me Kyle's post again."

I unlocked my phone and found Kyle's story. When I tapped it, the Help Me image appeared, but something new had been added to his story. It was a screenshot of an iPhone. The wallpaper was black and the only icons on the phone were for the various social media outlets Brand Nue expected us to use. I recognized it immediately because it was just like the one I'd been given when I accepted the temp job.

"Kyle added something," I said.

Maybe I'd been wrong. Maybe everything was okay. Maybe this had all been a stunt, just like Loncar suggested.

I magnified the screen and moved it around with my index finger. There was nothing interesting or fashionable about the screen shot. Nobody would think twice about this—or worse, they'd think it was an accidental post.

"What's it say?" Loncar asked. He leaned forward.

I held up my hand to quiet him and examined the image. What was the point of this? What was it Kyle wanted me to know?

And then I saw it, in the upper right-hand corner, so small and seemingly insignificant I almost didn't take notice. His battery was at one percent.

His phone was about to die.

The story had been updated in the time that I spent with Loncar. That meant his phone might not be dead yet. I launched the Find Me app and saw a bunch of blue dots in the area.

Every blue dot was an influencer employed by Brand Nue. "One of these blue dots is Kyle," I said. "His battery is at one percent. When his phone dies, he's on his own."

"Can you call him?"

I held up my burner. "This phone is owned by Brand Nue. They can track anything I do on it. And if he's down to one percent, the last thing we want to do is force him to use it up with a call. We don't know if he's getting an internet signal or if he's using data. Location services eats up a lot of battery. Kyle must know that. He wouldn't do this if he wasn't getting desperate."

I set the phone down and we stared at the dots. One of them was the only connection I had to someone I'd met at a trying time in both of our lives and never expected to see again. A stranger who'd become a friend through a temporary job and a shared love of the fashion industry.

"Come on, Kyle, I know you're out there. I know you need my help. Which dot is you?" I needed something—a sign, a message, anything. And then, one of the blue dots vanished from my screen.

11

TALK TO ME

"WHAT HAPPENED?" LONCAR ASKED.

"His phone died," I guessed. I picked up my phone again and moved the screen around. The app updated in real time and the dots moved slightly.

"Talk to me," Loncar said.

"I don't have time to talk to you," I said. I shoved my phone into my handbag and stood up. "Kyle Trent is out there with no connection to the world. That update will keep his Instagram story live for another twenty-four hours, but if his phone is off, then he's got nothing. He doesn't even know I'm trying to find him."

Loncar tapped the pen a few more times and then set it down on the desk. He looked up at me from under drawn eyebrows, and while I knew his resting face bordered on cranky-old-man, I also knew he recognized a call for help when he saw one.

"I'll take the case. Go home and send me everything you can about Kyle Trent. Until I know more about your employer, don't tell them we spoke. In fact, get me anything you can about them. You sign a contract?"

"Yes." I sighed.

"Get me that too. I want to know what you agreed to when you took this job."

Didn't we all.

WHEN MO PULLED into the driveway of my house, I was surprised to find a white pickup truck already there. The truck belonged to Nick, whose schedule had been unpredictable since he put his business on indefinite hold.

Trouble with his company had led him to question his future and he'd taken a hiatus from fashion while he figured things out. Six months ago, he'd been inspired by the athletic shoe business, and a month-long trip to Asia had sealed the deal. He returned with a suitcase full of samples and a fascination with the differences between the sneaker and stiletto trades.

I'd watched his malaise after losing his business morph into passion as he planned out the launch of Saint Nick. (He originally wanted to call it "Nick's Kicks," but confusion with the "Knicks" led to a name change. You gotta pay attention to things like search engine optimization, I'm told.)

Nick had a calming effect on me. Just being in his space helped me rein in my active imagination and recognize when I was jumping to conclusions. He was yin to my yang, common sense to my crazy, and peanut butter to my chocolate. Nick might be the perfect person to help me organize my thoughts.

I paid Mo and ran into the house. "Nick?" I called. When he didn't answer, I went upstairs. The door to the bedroom was almost closed but not quite. As I approached the door, I heard Nick's voice behind it. "You need to calm down, okay? I didn't know she was coming home either. Maybe you should just hide in the closet until I get rid of her."

Calm down? Hide in the closet? Rid of her?

Her? Who her?

Was I her?

I pushed the door open.

"What are you doing here?" Nick said. Get out!" He crossed the room and slammed the door in my face.

12

MARRIAGE COUNSELOR

THAT WAS NOT THE CALMING EFFECT I'D HOPED to feel upon finding Nick home.

"Kidd?" Nick said through the door. His voice was tentative. "Are you still there?"

"Yes."

"What are you doing home already?"

"I could ask you the same thing."

"Hold on."

I backed away from the door and sat on the top step of the staircase. Logan wandered up the stairs and walked back and forth, rubbing his fur against my pleated skirt. I'd never wanted to change my clothes more.

The bedroom door eased open and Nick came out. He pulled the door shut behind him. "Hi," he said. "Did you hear any of that?"

I nodded.

"I can explain."

I moved my eyes from his face to the door. Had I missed something? Was there a woman in there? Was Nick cheating on me? Was this how marriages fell apart?

I stood and scooped up Logan. His black fur pressed against my red sweater and he looked up at my face. "Meow," he said. He turned his head and looked at Nick and meowed at him too.

Our own feline marriage counselor.

Did we need a marriage counselor already? We'd only been married a little over a year!

"Who is she?" I asked.

"Who?"

I pointed at the door. "Her."

"Her who?" Nick asked again. He turned to look at the door behind him, and then turned back. "You heard me. You know. Don't be mad. I was going to tell you when the time was right."

I opened my eyes wide. "When would the time be right? You were supposed to be out working all day. I come home early and find you here in the bedroom with the door shut. You just told someone to calm down and you said you didn't expect me home yet. That sounds suspicious." Behind the door, I heard muffled crying. It was enough proof to send calm fleeing for the hills. "All I know is how this looks, and it looks like you're hiding a woman in the bedroom. *Our* bedroom."

Nick held his arm out, his hand open and reaching for mine. I looked down at it and didn't move. He stepped forward and took me by the wrist and pulled me toward the door. I leaned back with counter-resistance. I didn't want to go in there. I didn't want to meet his mistress face to face. I didn't want any part of his indiscretion.

He turned the doorknob and pushed the door wide open. A small black French bulldog sat in the middle of a sheet of wrapping paper with a slipper in its mouth. Its pointy black ears were longer than Logan's, and its eyes, nose, and mouth made a tiny pout in the middle of its face. Its eyes, round and glossy, stared back at me. It stomped its feet a few times and punched through the wrapping paper under comically disproportionate paws.

"Who's that?" I asked.

"According to you, that's my mistress."

"The puppy is a she?"

"Yes."

"Is she for me?"

"No. She's for my dad. He's all alone in that apartment and I thought he'd like some company."

My heart exploded with a warm, gooey sensation that flooded out my arms and legs.

As hard as it was to tear my attention away from the puppy, I did. I threw my arms around Nick and hugged him tight. "He's going to love her," I said. We pulled apart and stared at the funny black dog with the large pointy ears. She whimpered. Nick squatted down and ran his hand over her head.

"Are we good now?" I asked.

He stood. "As far as I'm concerned, we were never not good. Except it's a little disconcerting to learn you were that quick to assume I'd already taken up with a mistress." He leaned back against the bed and crossed his arms. "Have I done something to make you think I'm that kind of guy?"

"No. Of course not."

"But it didn't take much for you to get there."

"You know me, Nick. I jump to conclusions. I see a couple of things that seem odd and I come up with an entire narrative to fill in the gaps." I'd promised myself that things would be different, but so far, they were the same as always. "It's this social media thing. My job is to make it look like I'm having the time of my life at these events, and so far, I've managed to look scared, bored, embarrassed, and awkward."

"You never set out to be a social media influencer, and I doubt this is the job you're going to have for the rest of your life. But it's something, and something is better than sitting around on the sofa watching reality TV."

"I know. I'm just not used to being surrounded by so much inauthenticity. I'm more of a what-you-see-is-what-you-get type."

"Trust me on this. With you, you get a little extra."

"You're calling me extra?" That was one of the hashtags Brand Nue encouraged us to use at especially swank events.

"Something like that." Nick pulled me close

and put his arm around me. He kissed my forehead. "Kidd, you've given me a lot of reasons to worry about you in the past, but the one thing I'm not worried about is you falling into the phony life permanently. You've got a good sense of what you can and can't trust. The rest of the world might look at these posts and buy into the hype, but I bet if you took five minutes to examine them closely, you could pick them apart and know they're trying to sell you something."

Nick was right. I could. Why hadn't I thought of that? I knew every bit of fakery Kyle would use in his posts because I had access to the very same props. If I needed to understand what the last few days of his life had been life, all I had to do was check his social media feed.

"Kidd? I know that look. Five minutes ago, you thought I was cheating on you but now you're a million miles away. Talk to me. What are you thinking?"

"I'm thinking you're a genius." I tipped my head back and kissed him. "Finish wrapping my present and meet me in the kitchen."

"What makes you think I was wrapping your present?"

I smiled. "Once I got over the appearance of something I knew not to be true, I was able to see the facts. The only reason you'd be in here with the door closed the week before Christmas is for that."

This time Nick kissed me. "See? You're more insightful than you thought."

13

PERSPECTIVE

When I first took the job with Brand Nue, I'd gotten instructions on how to set things up so my Instagram posts fed directly into my Facebook and Twitter accounts. Kyle was the one who told me not to do that. "People can tell you're phoning it in," he said. "Post to both directly. Avoid hashtags on Facebook because they make your post look less personal. Use emojis whenever possible. And remember the golden rule: it doesn't matter how flattering your picture is, it only matters if it stops people from scrolling through their feeds."

Kyle was the master at getting people to stop scrolling. He'd had a lifetime of things handed to him on a platter, and until the day he lost his fiancé, he hadn't had much of a struggle in life. He even used the hashtag #toxicmale without irony and his follower count only grew. Kyle Trent, to the rest of the world, was who women wanted to be with and men wanted to be.

It was no wonder Brand Nue signed him. And if I were to understand what Rosha told me, Kyle was exactly the type to leverage his social media following into something bigger and better. This was a distraction for me, but for him, it was a stepping stone.

That put things into perspective.

I pulled up his Instagram page and checked his story. The same one, the *Help Me* post, was still there. The countdown clock had been reset when he added the screenshot, but a few hours had passed since then. Unless another update was added, the story would vanish in twenty-two hours.

I had less than a day to find Kyle or else.

Or else what? It wasn't lost on me that this literal cry for help was made on social media. I'd be a fool to think I was the only person who saw it.

I clicked over to Kyle's profile page. His follower count had grown by over a hundred thousand followers since I'd last checked. People were watching. People were interested in what he had to say. People were waiting to see what happened next.

Were any of them doing what I was? Looking for clues to where he was or what had happened? It didn't seem so. Kyle was either playing a high stakes game of wolf crying, or he was a victim of his own hype.

I dug my burner phone out of my handbag and sent him a message: *You avail for a meet-up later today? Still need to get that sneaker pic.*

The text showed up green. His phone was offline or dead. Rule one of Brand Nue was to keep our burner phones powered up at all time. Our welcome packages came with two backup batteries and a power bank. I might not have read the whole contract, but I'd read that.

The green text did not inspire confidence. I called Eddie.

"This better be good. I just started *Bad Santa.*"

"I need a favor."

"Dude, you always need a favor."

"And you're always happy to oblige, right? Because you know my heart is in the right place."

"Sure. We'll go with that."

"How about I make a thousand-dollar donation to the skateboard park?"

"What do you need?"

"Text Kyle on his personal phone and ask

him something you would normally ask him. Don't mention me, don't mention Brand Nue, and don't mention anything you wouldn't want plastered in the internet."

"Dude, you're the one who agreed to display your life on the internet. I'm the picture of privacy."

"Sure, we'll go with that," I said. "Just do it and call me back when you're done."

I hung up and waited. Seconds later, a text showed up from Eddie. *Text bounced. You happy?* A second text followed. *Make check payable to Ribbon Skates.*

I hung up and made two notes in my financial ledger—*Loncar/sofa; Eddie/Skateboard park—$1000*—and then turned my attention to Facebook. Unlike other influencers, Kyle used a different set of images here. Instead of showing off carefully staged product shots, on Facebook he was a guy's guy. Throwing a football with his bros, rubbing the fur of his dog, stretching out before a run, chugging water after a run. Late night snack from a 24-hour convenience store.

There was something for the ladies, too. Hair rumpled after waking up in tossed sheets. Shirtless, of course.

Just a regular guy.

The pictures were great in terms of making him look approachable. You felt like you were in his world, in his gym, in his house. In his bed.

Who had taken these pictures? Someone who was with Kyle in his bedroom.

Candi?

Leaving Kyle's IG feed up on my tablet, I searched for @HardCandi on my old laptop. There she was. I hadn't met Candi. I'd only talked to her on the phone. But this woman fit the description Loncar had provided. This was her.

The woman in the picture had long,

tousled pink hair that faded into platinum at the ends. Both of her bare shoulders were decorated with colorful tattoos of wrapped pieces of candy. A row of small silver hoop earrings, at least seven of them, lined the curve of her ear, but unlike Rosha, no other piercings interrupted her face. Her tan skin contrasted with the silky sheets of the bed, as did her short, red fingernails. She sold a just-woke-up style and included #unretouched in her list of hashtags. I wondered how many trips to the salon it took to get her ready for her close-ups.

Two thirds of the way down the page, in a post that prominently featured an expensive pink champagne from a product launch that took place before I joined Brand Nue, was a picture of a woman in a bed identical to the one on Kyle's Facebook feed.

I compared Candi and Kyle's posts. Kyle in the gym matched Hard Candi promoting a new line of workout wear.

Kyle rubbing the fur on the dog had the same carousel in the background that Candi stood on while drinking the latest new designer water. Kyle limbering up for a jog matched Candi laying out in a bikini. (If she was promoting a product in that picture, the client should ask for their money back.)

I had to give them credit. They must have coordinated the placement and timing of their posts.

It was the same principle Kyle had taught me. Actually—not quite. His and my posts were together. Two friends who got invited to the most exclusive of parties running into to each other and mugging for the camera. As far as I could tell—and I went all the way back to April—there were no pictures of Candi and Kyle together.

Like everything else here, that had to be by design.

After ten minutes of analyzing their

photos, I knew one thing. I had to talk to Candi.

Foolishly, I hadn't gotten her number when she answered Kyle's phone this morning, and I didn't want to rely on a direct message that would be too easy to ignore. It was almost six o'clock, and because it was dark out, it felt like eight. I called Brand Nue, hoping they, like the rest of the world, were working extended hours for the holidays.

Rosha answered. "Hey, Sam, what's shaking?"

"I was hoping you could put me in touch with Candi. We talked about coordinating efforts for the Kickin' It party, but I haven't heard from her yet."

"Don't tell me she went missing too?"

It was unclear from her tone whether this was intended to be humorous. I bit back a reply that things had gotten more serious and a detective was involved and forced a laugh. I reached for the tablet and scrolled to the most recent post. Thirteen minutes ago Candi posted a picture of her applying red lipstick. “She’s right there on Instagram.”

“I was kidding! You’re the most serious of our clients, you know that? It’s funny. Hold on.” Rosha put me on hold and the Bing Crosby/David Bowie version of “Little Drummer Boy” entertained me until she returned. “You’re in luck. Looks like Candi’s at home.”

“How do you know that?”

“She lives in those new apartments behind the outlets, you know, the ones that cheaped out on the renovation and are being sued?”

“What makes you think she’s there?”

“The Find Me app. I monitor all the influencers.”

“Do you know where I am?”

“You’re at home now, but earlier today you were in the field like everybody else,” she said. “You still don’t get it, do you? With this job, your every move is public. Brandon spent a fortune on a profile report of mind-mapping, decision-making, and influential behavior. Based on your last week of posts, he can predict your whole day before you even get out of bed."

14

IN THE CONTRACT

From the moment I accepted this job, I pushed the Big Brother aspect of it out of my head and focused on one thing: free product. The anonymous windfall eliminated my usual concerns about money, but I was only human. Kyle, having a similar background to mine in fashion retail, knew exactly which buttons to push when it came to pitching the concept to me.

Free designer merchandise. Before it goes to market. Carte blanche in terms of styling. A chance to impact the success of a brand during the busiest time of the year.

There were three things I loved: solving problems, helping people, and getting free fashion. Accepting a job where I combined all three was a no-brainer.

There was a reason Eddie turned down Kyle's offer and recommended me.

"Is there any way you can get a message to Candi for me?" The phone was silent. "Hello? Rosha?" I pulled the phone away from my head and checked the screen to see if the call had dropped. "Hello?" I said again.

"Why don't you want to call her yourself?"

"I don't have her number."

"Yes, you do. All influencer phone numbers were in the orientation package that came with your signed contract."

Hold up.

"Isn't that a violation of privacy? For you to give those numbers out?"

"Sam, we own those numbers and those

phones. We supply the necessary equipment for you to do what you need to do. It's in our best interest to get you out there, together or separate, flooding your social media accounts with images from our clients. There's a reason it's a violation of company policy for you to use your own equipment. If somebody quits or gets fired, it's a simple data transfer to get their content and repurpose it or hook up a new influencer. It's all right there—"

"—in the contract," I supplied.

"Yes." There was a slight pause on the other end of the phone before she spoke, this time in a voice barely above a whisper. "You have no idea how refreshing it is to talk to somebody who read the contract. We've had so many problems, Brandon's keeps a contract law office on speed dial."

Of course, he did.

We said goodbye and I pulled my earbuds out and set the phone on the table. "Hey, Nick?" I called up the stairs.

The bedroom door opened. "Yes?"

"There's a package on the nightstand on my side of the bed. Can you bring it down when you're done?"

"I'm done. Hold on." A few seconds later, he appeared at the top of the stairs. The black French bulldog waddled closely behind his feet. "What's this? My Christmas present?"

"It's my contract for Brand Nue."

His eyebrows dropped over his root-beer-barrel-colored eyes and his mouth turned down at the edges. "This package hasn't been opened. Didn't you read the contract before you started?"

"No! I didn't read the contract, okay?" I grabbed the package from him and tore it open. From inside, I extracted a bound stack of papers filled with sentences only a person with bionic vision could read. "Who has a seven-hundred-page contract for a temp job?" I dropped the stack and it landed on the hardwood floor with a *thud.* Logan trotted out from the kitchen and sniffed the paper. The bulldog whimpered at the site of him. Logan, aware of the dog for the first time, left the contract behind and walked up the stairs. He leaned in and sniffed the bulldog, who sat completely still aside from her little, wagging tail. When Logan was done with his inspection, he walked past the puppy to the bedroom. The puppy turned away from Nick and followed.

Nick jogged down the stairs. "Their contract is seriously seven hundred pages long?"

I bent down and grabbed it and carried it to the sofa. I sat down and flipped to the last page. "I stand corrected. It's only six ninety-two."

Nick sat next to me and took my hand. "Sounds like seven hundred to me."

I leaned back against the cushions, tipped my head back, and closed my eyes. "What have I gotten myself into? These people know every move I make. They know where I am. Between my posts, backgrounds, and location services, they know when I go to the bathroom."

"They probably know how many times a week you go to the pretzel outlet. Even I don't know that."

I jabbed Nick lightly in the ribs. And then, because he hadn't criticized my negligence regarding the Brand Nue contract, I added, "Five."

"Five what?"

"Five times a week. I usually stop in sometime after breakfast for a snack from their sample table."

"They don't mind you eating their samples every day?"

"Are you kidding? I'm their best customer. Sometimes they serve me the experimental pretzels that just came out of the oven."

"Too bad the pretzel companies never hired Brand Nue. I can't begin to imagine what you'd do if you were being paid to promote product you already loved."

Nick was right. So far, I'd only faked my way through jobs, because everything about social media influencing felt fake. I made special outfits to match my posts, used Perfect 365 to airbrush my face, and applied filters to my images. None of that was real. None of that was authentic.

But if I loved a product, if I really loved it, I'd be extra. Followers would know what lit my fire because they could tell. People weren't inherently stupid, it was social media that treated them as though they had no opinions of their own. There was a reason some posts went viral and, unless they featured a surprise celebrity product launch, it was because they touched a nerve. People wanted to care about something.

I was going to make them care about Kyle.

15

CAT VIDEOS

If the entire world I was tasked to inhabit was about getting attention, then I had an entire world at my disposal. I searched through my recent pictures, found one of me with Kyle, and wrote a caption: *Living the fabulous life with fashion friend @TheRealKyleTrent outside Pop Shop in West Ribbon. Kyle gets around! Repost for a chance to win an #UglyChristmasSweater or something better. (what's better than an ugly Christmas sweater???)* I posted it with the hashtags #WhereIsKyleTrent? and #repost. I repeated with pictures from every event we'd attended over the past week with corresponding prizes for each. I was hoping a little bit of postage would go a long way.

I went upstairs and changed out of my ivory sweater and gold skirt and into a Christmas sweater, short, red plaid skater skirt, and thigh high red patent leather boots. It wasn't the most practical outfit I'd worn, nor the most blend-in-y, but I was tired of being caught on photo looking less than Instagram ready. I was Kim Kardashian getting froyo in Yeezy sweats at four a.m. Of course, I ran errands in red patent leather thigh high boots. Doesn't everybody?

It wasn't like being an influencer was the first time I'd ever posted to social media. Like the rest of the world, I kept in touch with friends in different cities and states through Facebook updates and the like. I'd even posted a video of Logan scaling the Christmas tree last week, my version of giving back to the universe of social media that had given me unlimited cat videos.

In the three years that I'd been back in Pennsylvania, my life hadn't exactly been worthy of updates. I'd gotten involved in one criminal investigation after another, and nothing about that felt like cause for a post. Did people want to know that I found my boss dead in an elevator? That I helped bust open a knockoff ring or helped catch an arsonist?

Sure, that all sounded good, but it was only half of the story. I'd been knocked out, shot at, beaten up, chased, threatened, and forced to wear sweatpants. I'd put the lives of people I loved in danger. I'd moved out of New York and back to the town where I grew up to trace my life backward and find the point at which I traded happiness for career success, and then made timid advances to try to have both.

And here I was. Financial freedom had found me. So had love. But still, I was sitting in my kitchen, worrying about a friend for no reason other than my gut told me something was wrong.

"What does the rest of your night look like?" I asked Nick.

"Now that your present is wrapped, my night is all clear." He winked, and then his face changed, from playful to panic. "The dog," he said. He jumped up from the kitchen chair and then took the stairs two at a time and turned to the bedroom. "No, dog, no. What did you do?"

The next series of sounds told me one thing: Nick's night was no longer open.

Nick returned with the puppy under one arm and a leash wrapped around the other. "Correction: I'm going to take this girl out for a walk and then get you a new present to replace the one that *someone* destroyed."

I stood up. "I love you, Nick, and I don't need a present under the tree to know you love me too." An idea blossomed in my brain, and I couldn't believe I hadn't thought of it sooner. "There is one thing I want. You can't wrap it or put it under the tree, but it's a present only you could give."

He leaned down and kissed me. The dog turned her head and whined. "What do you want, Kidd? A pizza? A custom pair of shoes? A romantic getaway to Italy?"

I studied his face and considered what I was about to ask. "I want you to hire Brand Nue to run a last-minute social media blitz for you."

Nick stepped back. The puppy wriggled in his arms and Nick set her down and clipped on the leash. The puppy stretched the leash toward the door, but Nick stayed where he was. He didn't immediately ask why or offer the factual evidence that he had nothing for them to promote, both of which would have been totally normal responses.

Nick was smart. He didn't need to ask why or tell me he had nothing to promote. We were past needing to exchange normal responses.

"Do they know we're married?" he asked.

"Probably, but not because I told them," I said. "I got the job through Kyle's recommendation, and I told him to keep you out of it. Your business is yours, and sometimes drama follows me. I didn't want to do anything that would negatively impact you."

Nick pulled me in and hugged me tight. "You're amazing, Kidd." I rested my head against Nick's chest, and we stood that way for a few minutes while the dog wound her leash around our legs. "This right here is why I'll do whatever you ask. Because what you're asking for isn't about you. It never is."

While Nick took the puppy out for a walk around the block, I made a plan. First things first: get info on Kyle to Loncar.

What did I know about Kyle? What the rest of the world knew about him. What he posted on social media. I may not have been able to recreate his past twenty-four hours for the former detective, but I could recreate any other window of time in the missing man's life because it was all right there.

It was all right there.

Why hadn't I thought about that before?

Kyle was using his burner phone to send out his message of help. He didn't have his personal phone; Candi did. But he was burning a bridge with his Insta Story and screenshot. No retail client or designer wanted to see that stuff, and the lack of hashtags indicated that wasn't the motivation behind Kyle's post.

I pulled his Instagram feed up on my tablet and scrolled through the pictures backward until I found one from the first party we'd attended together. I noted the location, time, and identifiable people in the picture with Kyle, in this case, me. I repeated the summary for every picture between then and now.

An interesting pattern developed. The first three pictures Kyle posted from each event were alone. Him arriving. Him entering the event. Him posing with product. Next was a shot of the party scene, a funny selfie with merriment in the background. Last was a picture of him posing with another influencer.

Leon.

16

CHARMING

EVERYTHING I'D LEARNED ABOUT LEON AND Kyle was that their relationship was contentious. This post indicated otherwise. What was the real story? Were they friends who played up a competition between them for online drama, or were they arch enemies who existed to one-up each other?

Worse, how was I to know?

NICK RETURNED HOME with a white pizza, my current obsession. He'd had the foresight to ask them to add diced tomatoes and basil leaves: his not-so-subtle drive to increase my vegetable intake.

I chose to see this as charming.

I bit into a slice and examined the photos in Kyle's Instagram feed. There were five pictures for each event, scattered over a four-hour window. A social media blitz for each event. In between these bursts were lifestyle images that could have been taken at any time and used in his updates to fill time between bookings. I was less interested in them than I was the event photos for one reason.

The selfies didn't just capture merriment in the background. They captured the other attendees. The extreme magnification blurred a lot of the details, but fortunately for me, I knew what—or who—I was looking for. Anybody from Brand Nue.

The company managed our assignments,

and it came as no surprise that different people were booked for different gigs. Competing events and aligned profiles were the main reason. You couldn't be in two places at the same time, and most products benefitted from having the *right* endorsement, not just a bunch of endorsements.

It was this latter reason that explained the reason Brand Nue was so eager to hire me this close to Christmas. Even with a relatively small follower count, my background as a buyer and subsequent positions in the industry taught me how to communicate about trends and style. I knew what would speak to the target audience for a cashmere sweater priced over four hundred dollars or a pair of shoes with silver spikes up the back of the heel. I recognized that rose gold was the It metal of the season, and I knew the colorful $2.99 pashminas that some savvy soul had stocked at the local grocery store were among the best buys in the city.

My audience was enthusiastic, and my posts were reposted. For a temporary hire, I was a dream. But compared to the regulars, I was strictly amateur hour. Studying the posts on Kyle's page was like taking a masterclass in social media. Even with the tips he'd given me during the days where I shadowed him, I got distracted by the expert composition of most of his shots more than once.

The puppy whimpered by the sofa until Nick lifted her and set her on a pillow. She rolled onto her back and promptly fell asleep with her paws in the air. I didn't know where Logan was, but I suspected he'd take issue with this blatant display of cuteness.

"How's it going?" Nick asked.

"I noticed a pattern in Kyle's posts, and now I'm going through them to see who else I can identify from Brand Nue.

"You really think this has something to do with the publicity firm you work for?"

"I do. Don't you?"

"I'll defer to you on this. Walk me through what you know."

I loved when Nick wanted to help!

I leaned back and angled the laptop screen so Nick had a better view and pointed at a tattooed woman in the background of the pictures taken from a party last week.

"Hard Candi answered his personal phone, so she's intimate enough with Kyle to feel comfortable doing so. How'd she get it? Did he leave it at her house the night he went missing? Or did she steal it from him?" I jotted down notes. "Loncar knows her, too. He said she's a repeat offender who's been in and out of the system since she turned eighteen."

"For what?"

"Misdemeanors. Nothing that put her into felony territory. Either she's smart or lucky."

"Who else?"

"Neon Leon. He's easy to spot because he always wears neon." I tapped blurred blobs of chartreuse, electric blue, highlighter pink, and acid green in the background of different photos. "I was at Brand Nue when he showed up to argue about getting fired, and it sounded like his jobs all went to Kyle. Those product endorsements are a whole other thing at their level."

I reached for my contract and flipped through the pages. I located "endorsement and compensation" behind "filters", "best times to post", and "suggested poses to maximize body angles." What I saw changed everything.

"Those assignments that moved from Leon to Kyle are worth twenty grand each." I kept my hand on the page and looked up at Nick. "That's a hundred thousand dollar windfall the week before Christmas. Leon would have ample motive to keep Kyle from fulfilling those expectations."

"No joke," he said. "A windfall like that can change your life."

We were silent while the new information, a possible motive for someone to target Kyle, sank in. Nick was right. A six-figure windfall could change your life.

Nick and I hadn't talked about the anonymous payout that I'd been paid. I considered it ours, though every time I'd mentioned that, he waved me off and said it was mine. I'd offered to invest in Saint Nick, but he said no to that too. Knowing I had that money calmed that normally frantic aspect of my life, and I wasn't in a rush to spend it.

Nick stood behind me with one hand on the back of my chair and the other on the dining room table. He leaned down and studied the screen. I felt his closeness and rested my head against his arm. He bent down and kissed the top of my head.

I looked up at him. "What would you do with a six-figure windfall?"

"I'd move my dad from the apartment into a retirement home. I'd fly to Asia and find a warehouse to produce samples of some of my sketches. I'd buy Logan that catnip toy that looks like a fish. And I'd take you on a romantic getaway to wherever it was you wanted to go."

"None of that is for you."

"All of that is for me," he said. "When the people I love are happy, I have everything I need in life."

Nick's attitude on gratitude and generosity were something I aspired to feel. For too long, I'd chased dreams that were center to me. My happiness. My bank account. My upgraded pretzel-of-the-month club.

But I couldn't help see that Nick, for most of the time that I'd known him, was happy, and I, for most of the time I'd known me, was still seeking something.

I stood up and wrapped my arms around him. "I'm glad we can talk about this stuff," I said.

"We can talk about anything."

"Except Christmas presents," I added.

"You can talk about Christmas presents all

you want. Just don't try to trick me into giving anything away."

"I don't want to even think about presents until I figure this out."

"Are you any closer?"

"Not really. Candi and Leon could both have reasons to have done this. Maybe Rosha posted that story from the office to drum up some drama, or one of Kyle's clients tossed him a bonus incentive to do it. Or maybe this is all my active imagination. Candi is the one who told me Kyle was missing. Would she do that if she's the one who offed him?"

Nick stifled a smile.

"And Leon brought a prop gun to Brand Nue and staged a photo using their lobby cameras. That's a little too on-the-nose for someone who has something to hide."

"What about Brandon Nue? He's the connection between all these people right?"

"Yes, but Brandon stays behind the scenes. I've gone through Kyle's last thirty posts and analyzed the backgrounds and Brandon's not in one of them. He hires us to do this work while he focuses on bringing in new business."

"Speaking of that," Nick said. "There's no way I can hire Brand Nue without people connecting them back to you."

He handed me his phone. On the screen was a solicitation email from Brandon himself, introducing the company and laying out what he could offer should Nick find himself in the market for a publicity firm. It was a standard business move and I should have seen it coming.

"Do you have any other ideas?"

I did. A big one. And it was going to take a Christmas miracle to pull it off.

17

PLAN B

THERE WERE TWO PEOPLE I COULD THINK OF asking to pose as potential clients for Brand Nue. One was Eddie. His involvement with the local skateboard park was enough to give him credibility in terms of needing to raise the profile of his project, and leveraging the needs of a non-profit might be just the thing to get Brandon to take him on at a reduced rate this time of year. Besides, fundraising a project like this would get Brand Nue in front of a whole bunch of people, starting with the sneaker crowd, ending with the skateboard crowd, and touching the parents of everyone in the middle. There's no way Nue would say no.

But just in case, I had a plan B.

I'd promised to deliver materials to Loncar, and everybody knows favors are harder to refuse when requested in person. I unwrapped the dress shirt I'd bought Nick for Christmas (not even close to being the perfect gift) and put my almost-seven-hundred page contract inside. I added printouts of my notes regarding the three days of Kyle's life before he went missing and the identification of every other player involved. It was a thorough bit of investigation for an afternoon, but I still didn't know if I was on the right track.

I left my burner phone at home, thwarting the efforts of anyone tracking my activities. With about ten pounds of paper in a bag, I borrowed Nick's truck and drove back to Loncar's office. Geri was knitting the world's smallest scarf. She appeared startled by the sound of the door opening.

"You're back," she said. "We don't get a lot of repeat customers in one day."

I set my bag down and rotated my shoulders in backward circles to loosen them up. I glanced down at her desk and saw a small pile of similar knitted items. "See? It's a compulsion. I get bored, I knit."

"Is it me, or are they very, very small?"

"They're for babies. I get the yarn from second-hand cashmere sweaters. I tried to make a real scarf, but they take too much yarn and the cost outweighs the profits."

I picked one up. "Do you make a lot of money from them?"

"I'm working here, aren't I?" She smiled and turned her head toward Loncar's office. "Dad? Samantha's here to see you," she yelled.

The door to the office opened and Loncar stuck his head out. "I told you to use the phone." He looked from her to me.

I followed him into his office and held up my bag of paperwork. “Merry Christmas,” I said. I pulled out the box and set it on his desk.

“You got me a present?”

I lifted the lid and pushed the box closer to him. “I brought you everything I know about Kyle Trent, along with my contract.”

Loncar ran his thumb over the stack of paper in the box. “You read this thing?”

“I’m not going to dignify that with a response.”

Loncar flipped the first couple of printed pages off the stack and read the top one. After a few pages, he looked up.

“What was in this job for you?”

“I told you—free merchandise.”

He shook his head. “You said you had money. If that’s true, you could buy any of the merchandise these people offer you.”

“I still need a present for my husband. I thought spending time with influencers and tastemakers would give me an edge, maybe help me find out about some fantastic new thing he doesn't even know exists that would be perfect."

"You're doing all this for a gift idea."

"For the first time since Nick and I got together, I can afford to buy him the kind of present he deserves, and I can't figure out what that present should be."

"Maybe you should make him a home-cooked meal."

"I want to give him a present, not food poisoning. Nick knows I don't know how to cook."

"My point is maybe what he wants isn't something you can learn about from influencers."

I knew Loncar was right. I knew it just like I knew Kyle was in trouble. There are things you understand from the second you hear them, thoughts that seem easy to discount but resonate deep in your soul. Nick didn't want a new sweater or electronic gear. He didn't want a home cooked meal, either. He wanted to start a family.

It was something we'd discussed briefly when I thought I might be pregnant, and although I wasn't, it sparked the conversation about that being in our future. I hadn't spent time thinking all that much about it up to then, and now it seemed it was always in the back of my mind.

Nick was my partner. He was my best friend. I trusted him with my life. I saw how he cared about his dad. I saw how he cared about his business. I saw how he cared about Logan. I had zero doubts about what kind of father he'd be.

It was me I was worried about.

One could make the argument that I didn't take the influencer job to find the perfect gift for Nick, but that I took the job to avoid thinking about the one thing he wanted.

Loncar picked up the pages he'd removed

from the box and set them back inside. He closed the box. “I guess I know what I’ll be doing tonight. You need anything else?”

“There is one more thing.”

Loncar watched me. I wish I’d sat when I first arrived, but it felt wrong to make myself comfortable when I was on the verge of being thrown out. “I reviewed the case with Nick after I compiled that information, and all roads lead back to Brand Nue. I can keep an eye on Leon and Candi, but Brandon Nue is keeping an eye on all of us. That seems . . .”

“Against the law.”

I pointed to the contract. “No, apparently I agreed to the location monitoring when I signed the contract. But that’s the thing. Brandon knows a lot about all of us thanks to that contract and his ability to surveil us.”

“Like what?”

“How often he checks up on us. What level of detail he tracks. If he ever tries to match up our cellular activity with our social media feeds. That kind of stuff. We, well, we need someone on the inside to find out the extent of his knowledge."

"You said this earlier."

"I asked Nick. And he said yes. But then he thought about it and remembered that Brand Nue already tried to solicit his business. He's on their radar and there's no way they won't connect him back to me now."

Loncar glared at me and I held up my hands, palm-side out. "I also thought of Eddie Adams. He's fundraising for the new skateboard park and that makes for a perfect client. Social awareness, not-for-profit, community park. They need money, not sales. It's a feel-good project, and with the money Brand Nue is bringing in, they could use a tax deduction to offset their annual income. It's perfect."

Loncar relaxed into his chair. "It does sound perfect. Did Mr. Adams agree?"

"I don't know. Nick dropped me off here

and went to find him to ask. I can't imagine he'll say no. Kyle is more his friend than any of us and Eddie would want to help if he could."

I felt a buzzing sensation against my waist, and it took a moment to remember I'd shoved my cell phone into my coat pocket. I pulled it out and checked who was calling. It was Eddie.

"This is him. Hold on." I swiped the screen. "Are you in?" I asked. (With Eddie, it saved us a lot of time to just cut to the chase.)

"Yep, I'm in. I'm in up to my shoulders and when I hang up from this call, I'm going under."

"You're—what? That makes no sense. Did you talk to Nick? Did he tell you—ask you—did you guys work out a plan?"

"Dude, you're going to need a Plan B. There's no way I can help you with this."

"Why not?" I turned my back on Loncar and walked to the corner. I wasn't paying attention to where I walked and bumped my calf against a table. "What's so important that you'd rather do it than help out your friend?"

"It's not that I don't want to help, it's that I can't. Somewhere after *It's A Wonderful Life,* I snapped. Too much happiness. No stress. It's unnatural. I've spent the past twenty years around hostile customers and bitter sales associates. I had to go someplace that felt like the holidays."

"Where did you go?"

"The airport."

"Eddie, exactly where are you calling me from?"

"My hotel. In Florida."

18

ABSOLUTELY NOT

"YOU'RE IN FLORIDA?"

"Dude, you have no idea what forty-eight hours of holiday movies will do to the mind. Someone should do a psychological study."

"But we had breakfast this morning."

"Yeah, at eight o'clock. That was twelve hours ago. It's only a three-hour flight."

"What about Kyle?"

"What about him? He's probably avoiding that crazy Candi woman."

I forgot. Eddie didn't know anything about

what I'd learned so far. His marathon holiday movie schedule had precluded any contact from the outside world. I'd respected his wish and kept him out of it until we needed his help and apparently it was too late to ask.

"Did you talk to Nick?"

"About what?"

My phone buzzed with another incoming call. Guess who?

"Eddie, I gotta go. Nick's on the other line."

"Okay, dude. I gotta go too. Seaweed wrap in twenty minutes."

I juggled calls and accidentally hung up on Nick. I looked at Loncar. "There's a slight problem. Give me a sec." Loncar nodded and flipped another page of my contract while I called Nick back.

"Hi," I said when he answered. "I talked to Eddie."

"He's in Florida."

"I heard."

"We need another plan."

"I know."

We needed a plant inside Brand Nue. We all agreed on that. I couldn't do it. Nick couldn't do it. Eddie couldn't do it.

I turned toward Loncar and stared his plaid flannel shirt. No. It would never work.

"Kidd? Are you still there?" Nick asked.

"I'm putting you on speaker." I tapped the screen and set the phone on Loncar's desk.

Loncar looked up from the contract. "Is Mr. Adams on board?"

No. Mr. Adams was not on board, and unless there was some surfing in his future, he wasn't going to be on board the team that solved this particular problem. "Change of plans," I said. "Eddie's unavailable."

"Your powers of persuasion are slipping."

It was time to find out if that were, indeed, true.

Loncar crossed his arms over his chest. "Ms. Kidd, if you have an idea, I'd like to hear it."

My words came out in a rush. "Nick can't do it. Eddie can't do it." I kept my eyes pinned on Loncar's third button. There was no way I could make eye contact with him while thinking what I was thinking. "If only we knew someone who was completely unknown to the world of fashion, who could go in there, undercover, and hire Brand Nue on the spot. Someone who would know what to look for and what questions to ask. Do you have any suggestions?"

My phone made a sound, remarkably similar to the one Nick makes when he's trying to stifle a laugh.

"Dad, you should do it."

I looked up from Loncar's third button to see Geri standing in the door frame. "You said you wanted to change your life, so change your life. You lost fifty pounds after the divorce. You need a new look anyway."

"Absolutely not," Loncar said.

"Why not?" I asked. "You're an investigator.

I've read enough Sue Grafton books to know PIs sometimes have to pretend to be something they're not to get the info they want. You'll only go so far carrying around a clipboard."

Loncar and I had a bit of a stare-off, interrupted by a giant air bubble surfacing in the large blue water cooler that sat in the corner of the office. (Was there a water cooler in *The Maltese Falcon?* I think not.)

"You already know it'll work," I said. "And unless you've got a bunch of appointments lined up for the afternoon, I'm guessing your schedule is wide open."

Loncar picked up his pen and bounced the end of it on his desk. *Boink. Boink. Boink.* He pointed the pen at me. "If this is your idea of a joke, Ms. Kidd, I feel compelled to tell you we —" he gestured between us—"don't exist in joke territory."

I took offense. I rested my palms against the surface of his worn, wooden desk and leaned down. "I have *never* come to you with a joke. Our entire relationship is based on real, live, criminal activity. This time I came directly to you, which, I don't know, maybe you can credit to the spirit of the holidays." I tapped my phone. "Kyle Trent is in trouble and unless you have another idea, this might be his only hope."

The color drained from Loncar's face and it turned a ghostly shade of white.

"If we could send you in undercover, like a client looking to book us, you'd have access to everything: the tracking software, the recent assignments, the compensation of each of the influencers, and the clients. You're new to this world so nobody would think you were anything other than who you say you are."

"I can't inhabit your world without raising red flags. Undercover work is more nuanced than that and going in unprepared could do more damage than good. You need somebody who knows the lingo." He shook his head. "That's not me."

"What if you went in with a business partner?" I asked. "Someone who could cover all the bases you can't while you do the part you can?"

"You have someone in mind?"

I did. And I hoped this was one of those times Nick and I were thinking the same thing.

"I'll handle it," Nick's voice said.

Loncar seemed startled by the voice coming from my phone. He pointed to the device. "Is that Mr. Taylor?"

I nodded. "You think he'll say yes?"

"I think he'll jump at the chance," Nick said.

"Who?" Loncar asked.

"Nick's father."

"I'm on it," Nick said. The call disconnected.

I shifted my attention back to Loncar and

smiled. "You might want to close the office for the rest of the day," I said. "Because this time, you'll be in my world. Remember all those times you reminded me I know nothing about your job? Turnabout is fair play."

19

CONDITIONS

"TWO CONDITIONS," LONCAR SAID.

"Name them."

"My retainer is two thousand dollars in advance."

"Is that in addition to the sofa I offered to buy you?" Loncar glared at me. "Sure. Right. Two thousand dollars plus sofa. What's the other condition?"

"Somebody other than you takes me shopping."

I'VE NEVER BEEN SO happy to write a check in my life!

The details, though not completely worked out, involved Loncar and Nick Senior hiring Brand Nue for a last-minute campaign. The beauty of the skateboard park as fundraising client was off the table, but another business was on. Geri Loncar's tiny recycled cashmere sweater/scarves. We made one change to her business model: we turned them into accessories. Wrist Wrap: scarves for your wrist. They were the perfect item to promote on social media: eco-conscious, stylish, and the kind of thing you never thought you needed.

Loncar's makeover would prove trickier. I doubted Nick had the patience (or inclination) to take crabby old Loncar out shopping for the day, and with Kyle's clock possibly running out, we had to make it happen fast. Borrowing clothes would make the most sense, but Nick's clothes wouldn't come close to fitting.

Nick's dad's clothes would.

Nick Senior was the man who'd started the shoe company that Nick inherited, and thanks in no small part to some secrets in his past, he was also the reason Nick was on a possibly-permanent vacation from the footwear business. He'd been a part of the industry long enough to still talk the talk on occasion, but a broken hip kept him from walking the walk without a cane. It wasn't a stretch to think these two men could make this happen. Fast.

I flipped Loncar's Open sign to Closed while Geri stuffed small cashmere scarves into a plastic bag recycled from the local grocery store. I wasn't operating out of a desire for privacy. This entire plan hinged upon nobody knowing what we were up to, and that meant I had to act normal.

Rosha at Brand Nue had said all influencer phone numbers were in the contract, so while Geri taught her dad the highlights of the handknit scarf business, I flipped through the contract looking for contact info. Phrases like, "non-compete", "violation of terms", and "penalties beyond normal compensation" caught my eyes, but I squeezed them shut and remembered there was something more important than sales at stake. I opened my eyes and narrowed them enough to blur most of the words. The list of phone numbers was on page one hundred thirty-two. I dog-marked the corner and called Candi.

"Candi, it's Samantha Kidd."

"I know who this is. This is the f***in' number you called me from this morning."

"That's right. This isn't about Brand Nue, it's about Kyle. Do you have time to meet me somewhere?"

I BORROWED GERI'S CAR, an orange Kia Soul, and promised to return within the hour. I wouldn't have minded a less noticeable vehicle, but as I discovered while on the way, orange really was the new black—or silver, or beige. There were more orange cars on the road than I'd ever noticed before in my life.

We agreed to meet at Benedict's Eggs. I arrived first and sat at a booth close to the door. A dinner menu had replaced the breakfast one, but I stuck with coffee. A few minutes later, the doors opened and the woman from the photos, a little rougher around the edges without the help of her airbrushing apps entered. Her pink hair was covered with a black knit cap, worn loose with extra room on top of her head. She wore a gray motorcycle jacket over a T-shirt and tight, faded jeans. Both the collar of her T-shirt and the knees of her jeans were ripped out. I'd spent the morning freezing in my after-hours attire and had gone home to change. Candi appeared to be impervious to the temperature.

I held up my hand and waved and she approached my booth. "You're xoSamantha?"

"Yep."

She made no secret of her assessment of my Christmas sweater. "Have you heard from Kyle?" she asked. No "hello." No "Nice to meet you face to face." No "sorry I was rude the last time we talked and of course you're happily married and not interested in my boyfriend."

Perhaps I'd have to recalibrate my expectations.

"Not yet. Did you?"

"Just the f***in' Instagram story."

She slid into the booth and grabbed a stack of pink Sweet and Low packets from the container on the table. She lined them up and then tore them open and poured the contents directly onto the table. I watched as she fanned the sparkly crystals out from the pile and then jabbed her fingernail, red with green tip, into the substance and swirled it around.

Mabel, the waitress from this morning came over. “You ready to order, hon?”

“You’re still here,” I said, surprised.

“Double shift. My coworker went home sick. Don’t order the meatloaf. I’m pretty sure that’s what she had for lunch.”

“I’m sticking with coffee,” I said.

She turned to Candi. “How about you, sweetie?” She glanced at the sweetener on the table and pulled a pencil out of her apron and quickly swiped the crystals into a napkin, balled it up, and looked at Candi expectantly.

“Sweetie? What the f***. You’re like twenty-five.” Candi held her menu up. “I’m not eating here. Get me water, no f***in’ ice.”

Mabel, to her credit, did not respond. I made a mental note to tip her well.

I considered sharing my thoughts on the screenshot Kyle added to his story, the Find Me app that stopped working, and the solid investigative work that led me to confirm

Candi's relationship with him, but there was a nagging thought: What if?

What if Candi had Kyle tied up in her basement? What if she really was working a long con? What if she was absolutely nothing like the person she represented herself to be and I was following a trail of carefully doled out breadcrumbs?

I was keeping everything I knew to myself.

"Back to Kyle," I said. "I saw his Instagram story too. Is it possible this is all to increase his follower count before the Kickin' It party?"

"That's pretty f***in' cynical," she said.

"You know this world better than I do, and you've spent more time with Kyle than I have. I told you we planned to get photos at Pop Shop this morning. Him not showing was what bothered me, but maybe that's par for the course. I heard he got a slew of assignments that were initially tasked to Leon—"

"He did? Where'd you hear that?"

Think fast, Samantha. Stay vague. "The agency."

"Why'd you go there?"

I stared at the stack of paper in front of me. "I had a question about my contract."

"That contract is pretty f***in' thorough," she said. "I can't imagine what f***in' question you have that isn't easily answered by accessing the index."

There was an index?

"My contract is probably different than yours," I said. "I'm a temp hire. Holiday season only. I get fifty dollars per product campaign and I'm expected to post a minimum of six pictures for each product."

Candi made a sound of disgust. "Brand Nue is taking advantage of you and you don't even f***in' know it."

"I'm in it for the product. A couple of bucks isn't going to bother me."

"Don't be a f***in' moron. Kyle and Leon normally make twenty grand per endorsement. That number doubles for the holidays. That might be a couple of bucks to you, but not to me. Your acceptance of payroll inequality perpetuates the f***in' problem."

Candi was throwing around big numbers, the kind of numbers that affected normal decision-making skills. I'd been shocked to learn they made twenty grand per endorsement, but double? That was crazy money.

"I'm sorry they don't pay you your fair share, but that's on you, not me. This isn't my life's work. This time next week I'll go back to waiting in lines outside events like the rest of the residents of Ribbon while you're scheduling images to use between events."

"What are you talking about? My posts are legit. I don't f***in' pull that scheduling stuff like the rest of you."

"Candi, I checked your feed. I know your posts share a background with Kyle's, not at the same time, and with enough filters and photo editing tricks to keep most people from seeing it, but it's all right there. You and Kyle are practically living together."

"You don't know what you're talking about," she said. "Brand Nue keeps a furnished townhouse for us to use for lifestyle pics, but they also supply a f***in' tripod and camera. I've taken every f***in' one of my pictures myself."

20

ZERO CONFIDENCE

Did I believe everything Candi said? I didn't know. I'd been so confident about what I concluded after analyzing her Instagram posts compared to Kyle's and based on that intel alone had felt I was on to something. But if she was right, if Brand Nue kept a furnished townhouse for the influencers to use between pics, then it could be coincidence that both she and Kyle used the same backdrops.

Or, she could be lying to protect herself.

"Why don't I know about this townhouse?"

"Because you didn't read your contract."

Candi stood up. "This," she pointed her long, red and green French-manicured fingernail in the air and twirled it in a circle. "is a waste of time. If you need to reach me, go through Rosha. Don't contact me directly again."

"What about Kyle?" I asked.

"I have zero f***in' confidence in your ability to help him," she said. She made peace signs with each of her hands and held them against each other at a right angle, making a hashtag with her fingers. She tapped the fingers against each other twice. "Hashtag Zero," she said. The gesture felt hostile.

If I needed any proof that influencers weren't like the rest of us, I just got it. I finished my coffee, giving Candi time to put distance between us. If she were the one behind this, then I felt sure I'd rattled her cage. But if she weren't, then she was at as much risk as I was. More, probably, since I was just a temp.

I gave Candi time to get a head start,

generously tossed a ten-dollar bill on the table to cover my tab (and make up for Candi's rudeness) and left. It was after nine, and I was tired from a very long day. But every time I considered going home to crash, I thought about Kyle. If I fell asleep and something happened to him, I'd never forgive myself.

I was only a block from the spot where Kyle was supposed to meet me for our morning photo session. Had he gotten there after I left? Was there something there, some sort of cry for help or message that had seemed to fit the backdrop? There was one way to find out.

I left Geri's car in the Benedict's Eggs parking lot and walked down the block to Pop Shop. Pockets of people were on the street, heading toward their destinations or hovering outside shops. This was a busy street any time of the year, but this week the boutiques were open late, and the restaurants were overflowing with reservations. In two hours, when businesses were closed, the street would be dead.

I reached Pop Shop and pressed my face up against the window. A faint light in the back of the store provided the only illumination. I used the flashlight app on my phone to see more.

The interior had been cleaned up since the previous party. To the left of the cavernous room were stacks of shelves, piled recklessly high and ready to topple. Next to the shelves were chairs, and next to the chairs were rolls of colorful paper. They were the backdrops that Brandon provided to clients to hang to cover the walls if desired and change the interior into whatever it was they wanted it to be. Those must have been pulled out for tonight, since I already knew last night's party showed off exposed brick walls. There was movement by the back door. I strained my eyes to see who (or what—ick!) it was.

It was a person. A man. In a neon

sweatshirt, camouflage green army pants, and white, Nike sneakers.

Neon Leon was inside Pop Shop hours after being let go from Brand Nue.

When Brandon terminated him, he directed Rosha to cut off Leon's access. That meant key cards, phone access, the works. How did Leon get inside Pop Shop? He should have been frustrated, standing outside looking in like me.

As I watched, Leon hoisted a nylon backpack over his right shoulder and left out the back door. I hurried down the length of the building and turned onto the alley that ran behind the shop. Leon stood by the back door fussing with the locks.

"What are you doing?" I called.

Leon's head turned toward me. He squinted his eyes but said nothing. My heart was pounding in my chest. For a fleeting moment, I considered walking away. *No,* I thought. *Something isn't right here.*

I rubbed my hands together and approached the back door. “Leon, right?”

“Do I know you?”

“Samantha. Kidd.” I waited for recognition to cross his face. “xoSamantha on Instagram. I work for Brand Nue.” I paused again. How did he not recognize me? He pretend-shot me with a pantomime gun in the lobby of Brand Nue around lunchtime.

“You a spy for the boss man?”

“Spying?” I sort of was spying, but there was no boss man involved. “Wait. You mean Brandon? No, I’m not a spy. I’m an influencer. Like you.”

“How come I don’t know you?”

“I’m a temp. Holiday work. You really don’t remember me?”

“From where? Don’t tell me we met at a party. I don’t waste time on chicks at parties.”

This guy was charming—not. I was equal parts happy that our paths hadn’t crossed up to now and disgusted that a drop of his spittle landed on my cheek. I brushed it off with my gloved hand, making no effort to be subtle.

"I was at Brand Nue earlier today when you were fired. Brandon let you go over a post you made at the Mackenzie party. He told Rosha to cut off your access to the network. Does any of this ring a bell?" I waited for a reaction, but Leon just stood there glaring at me.

There are times when confrontation riles me up. More than once I've looked back on a moment and wished that I'd kept a cooler head. But this time, Leon's lack of response was the trigger. The adrenaline that coursed through my body when I first saw him gave me courage I might not have otherwise had in a dark alley with a man who brandished a gun. (To those of us who have had guns pulled on us in the past, toy guns are just as threatening as real ones.)

I stepped closer and jabbed my finger at his chest. "You were trash talking Kyle Trent, probably because you're mad that he got your assignments. But what you posted from the bathroom at the Mackenzie party was out of line and you know it."

His expression changed, from disinterest to surprise. His eyes widened and his mouth opened into a small, round O. "You know about that?"

"I know more than you think."

I knew nothing. Absolutely nothing. I didn't even know who Mackenzie was!

"I don't know what you're up to, Leon, but whatever it is you're doing here, you're done."

The surprise on his face shifted back to suspicion. "Nice act, sister, but you don't know she-eet," he said. "If you knew what happened at the Mackenzie party, then you'd know exactly why I'm here."

21

SOME DUDES CAN'T HANDLE THE PRESSURE

"I KNOW THE PICTURES YOU POSTED VIOLATED the terms of the contract," I said. "I know they were inappropriate and misrepresented Brand Nue. I know even though the client saw a thirty-seven percent sales increase, they told Brandon to let you go because it was more damaging to their brand to keep you on."

I was desperate. Regurgitating what I'd heard at Brand Nue hardly constituted knowing something, but if I'd learned anything from being an influencer, it was to act confident and pretend I was an expert. Just because Leon called my bluff didn't mean I had to stop bluffing.

Leon's shoulders fell. He balled up his fists and shoved them into the kangaroo pocket on the front of his neon hoodie. "It was an accident, man. That guy was never supposed to be in that picture."

"Who?"

"The Mackenzie owner. I'd been posting pics from the party all night and I needed a break from the crowd. I went into the bathroom and man, that was some good light. I posed by the mirrors and snapped a couple of pics. I didn't know he came out of the stall behind me with powder on his nose."

"You caught the owner doing coke in the bathroom of his own party?"

Leon shrugged. "Some dudes can't handle the pressure. He wasn't the first and he won't be the last."

"What did you say?"

"Nothing. He offered me some and I

refused. I don't get mixed up with drugs, yo. Messes with my temple." He bent his arms and flexed, and I made out the lines of muscles of his chest and arms.

"Go on," I said.

"I said I wouldn't say nothin' and he left. About an hour later, I asked Kyle to hold my phone. The next day social media accounts blow up. A picture of the owner of Mackenzie wiping his nose while coming out of a bathroom stall behind me shows up in my IG feed with the hashtag #busted."

"Kyle posted one of your pictures without you knowing? Why would he do that?"

"Sabotage, man. I get fired, he gets my gigs."

Kyle had told me at the holiday party that influencers were a cutthroat bunch. Had I completely misjudged him? Had he been talking about himself?

I had one more question. "Why didn't you

delete the images from your phone before you left the bathroom?"

"What good would that do? Those photos are backed up on the cloud. They'll exist forever." He made a gun sign with his hand again (this time with three fingers, not two) and tapped it on my shoulder. "It's all in the contract, man. Those M-Fers own our content for life."

There wasn't a whole lot I could say in response to that.

Leon left. There wasn't a lot I could do to stop him, and even less desire to keep him there. A few minutes after he walked away a neon motorcycle roared to live and sped down the alley.

I had an eerie feeling about the store, about Leon's presence at the store, and about what he'd been doing there. I pounded my closed fist on the door and kicked it too. The door opened from the inside. Brandon Nue looked as surprised to find me there as I was him.

"Samantha?"

"Brandon?"

"It's freezing out there. Come on in."

The interior temperature was warmer, but not by much. With Brandon were two men I'd seen around but hadn't formally met. They carried large white buckets and rollers and were dressed as though they were ready to tackle an HGTV home renovation.

Brandon gave the men painting and set-up instructions, then turned back to me. "We picked up a last-minute gig and I need to get the shop ready."

"Is that why Leon was here?"

Brandon tipped his head and closed one eye. It wasn't like he was winking at me—more like an assessment. "Leon? He's done. You were at the office when I fired him, remember?"

"I thought you might change your mind after he staged that shot in the lobby." As soon as I said it, I regretted it. Maybe Brandon didn't want me to know about the possibly illegal cameras in his lobby.

He laughed. "Did Rosha tell you about those cameras? My legal team wasn't on board with the concept and made me disable them to avoid lawsuits. I didn't bother with an announcement about the take-down because it would have let people know they were there."

"Just to clarify, they *weren't* mentioned in the contract? A couple of my pages were stuck together and I couldn't read them."

"They were in the original contract, but the legal team said it was too long and I had to cut it down."

There was an unabridged version?

Brandon located the breaker box and turned on the power. Lights flickered on, making it easier to see how much work had to be done to the interior to make it event ready. The easy clean-up had been taken care of: disposable champagne coupes and napkins had been tossed, the floor had been swept, and the trash had been emptied. Any clues I'd hoped to find had been whisked away with the cleaning service that Brandon kept on his payroll.

What I did find was a door. Behind the door was a staircase. And at the bottom of the staircase was a dirt-covered cellar. Hollywood scouts would have been thrilled to find such a spot; it was perfect for keeping a person in captivity.

There were no signs of a person being kept in captivity.

"What are you looking for?" Brandon asked, following me down the steps.

"Not what. Who. I'm looking for Kyle."

"Is that why you started that ridiculous #WhereIsKyleTrent? campaign? You still think some great mystery is taking place, don't you?"

"Kyle is a friend. I'm worried about him. And I'm grateful, honestly, I am. These jobs give me access to his world. Even if his disappearance has nothing to do with Brand Nue or one of your clients, just walking in his footsteps and learning what his life was like has to help on some level."

"Sam, the world of a successful influencer is seductive. That's how the good ones gain followers. You're close enough to our world to see the perks: free merchandise, invites to VIP events, airbrushed photos and everyone having the time of their life. You've worked for me for over a week now, and that's long enough to have seen how it works. My job with Brand Nue is to show people the illusion of perfection. We don't scratch the surface. We make everybody want what we have. That's what clients pay us for."

"I know. I get it."

"I don't think you do. Look around you. Where are you?"

"I'm at the pop-up store for tonight's event."

"You're in the basement on a floor made of dirt. To the rest of the world, this address is the hottest spot in Ribbon, but you're not the kind of person who accepts things at face value. You had to dig deeper, and here you are."

"I saw Leon come down here. I was at the front of the building, staring in the windows, and I saw him. He came in through the back, he went through that door," I pointed up the stairs—"and was gone or about a minute, then he came back and left out the back. He must have the key."

Brandon sighed. "Did he have a black nylon backpack with him?"

"Yes."

"That's his event bag. Styling products, change of clothes in case he gets a second gig. He probably stashed it here at the last party. Nothing out of the ordinary."

"I guess not."

"This isn't the first time your instincts

went opposite what's needed for this line of work."

I held up my hands. "Don't worry about me. I'm not looking to turn this into a full-time gig." In a way, it was refreshing to hear Brandon acknowledge the side of me that tended toward figuring things out. My inclination toward criminal cases had put me in dangerous situation after dangerous situation and had been a source of friction between me and Nick—until the criminal case involved him. That was a turning point for us.

Did this conversation represent the personal growth I constantly sought? If it was, then why did Brandon's words make me feel inadequate?

Brandon crossed his arms. "You don't get it, Sam, and I'm beginning to think you never will. The work we do has one purpose: promote our clients' product. Your instincts to use your assignments to 'help' Kyle are not only misguided, they violate the terms of your contract."

"I'm sorry. I won't—"

"I know you won't. Because you're done."

"Done?"

Brandon crossed his arms. "That's right. I'm letting you go." He extended his arm, an offered handshake intended to formalize what felt a lot like a termination. "Goodbye, Samantha. Best of luck in the future."

22

SURVEILLANCE

I LEFT OUT THE FRONT DOOR AND DIDN'T STOP to consider how dire things were until I was in Geri's Kia with the heater on full blast. I didn't care all that much about the job. Eddie had had the right idea: enjoy the holidays without the pressures of a job. I even had money. I could have Griswalded my house if I wanted. I didn't need this.

But it wasn't about me anymore. With Eddie out of town, I'd convinced Detective Loncar to pose undercover as a client for

Brand Nue so he could get inside and do his trained investigative thing. It was as good an idea as I'd ever had, and it was contingent upon me getting Brand Nue to take him on as a client.

Maybe Nick, his dad, and Loncar had gotten as far as I had. Maybe we were on square one. Maybe Kyle had found a phone charger and his location was back online.

Maybe Brandon fired me because he was the guilty party and I was getting too close to figuring him out.

I pulled out my phone and cued up Instagram. Kyle's story was still there. No updates. Nothing new on his feed. I searched for #WhereIsKyleTrent? and found hundreds of reposts of images he'd used over the past month. People were paying attention. At minimum, I hoped the activity would force someone's hand.

I clicked over to @NeonLeon. His latest

post, a pic of him in the gym was gaining traction. It had been posted about half an hour ago—the same time I would have sworn I saw him at Pop Shop.

It wasn't lost on me that social media, with its scheduling tools and interaction from followers, provided a canny way to manipulate timelines, provide alibis, and put people in two places at the same time. I'd heard stories about not-so-bright crooks who posted selfies with clues in the background, but how many more savvy sorts used the tools available to edit themselves from suspicion?

I called Geri. "I'm on my way back to the office with your car."

"Bring it over tomorrow," she said. "I took an Uber. I'm about to give the baby a bath and put her to bed. It would be a lot better for me if I didn't have to be available to let you in."

"Thanks, Geri. I owe you one."

I hung up and headed home. When I

arrived, the house was dark. I took off my thigh high boots and tossed them in a pile by the bottom of the stairs. The French bulldog sat in a large crate in the center of the room. He didn't seem to notice that there were bars between himself and the rest of the living room. Logan sat on the sofa nearby, his paws tucked underneath his body, his eyes focused on the dog.

Surveillance.

I said hello to the animals and went to the kitchen. My burner phone sat on the counter. When I lifted it from the counter, the screen lit up with notifications. Missed calls from Brand Nue.

Brandon probably wanted to make sure I knew I had to turn in the phone, and maybe even remind me that downloading data from it was a violation of my contract. I was almost relieved to be free of that paperwork.

I called the number back. Rosha answered.

"Samantha? Hey. You okay? I blew up your phone an hour ago."

"Sorry. I was with Brandon. Is there more paperwork to make things official? I'll come by the office tomorrow, if that's fine with you."

"I'm not calling about paperwork. I'm calling about a job. Brandon added a last minute booking to the schedule tonight. Are you free?"

It took a few seconds to process the mix-up. The job came into Brand Nue before Brandon canned me. Rosha called me immediately, but my phone was at home on the dining room table. Rosha and Brandon hadn't yet spoken so Rosha didn't know I was influencer non grata.

All we needed was for Loncar to get inside Brand Nue and check things out, which was even more important now that I had a new suspect. Brandon and Rosha were going to talk sooner or later, but right now, there was a window for our plan.

"I'm available. What's the gig?"

"It sounds crazy, but it'll be perfect for you. The company is Wrist Wrap. They're scarves for your wrist, handknit from repurposed cashmere yarn. They're not cheap, but with the right branding, they'll be perfect for the luxury set. The owners are two men who bought the inventory in a turn-key transaction."

This was it. The plan. Nick and Loncar had held up their end. I didn't care a whit about proving myself as an influencer, but this—this was life or death. I closed my eyes and turned my eyes in and up, focusing on the spot between my eyebrows. In meditation worlds, this was the location of my third eye.

I got dizzy. I opened my eyes and sat down. Two eyes were going to have to be enough.

"What's the dress code and location?"

"I'll send everything to your phone."

Was that smart? I didn't want to be trackable to anyone who worked for Brand Nue, but I also didn't want to tip anybody off.

"Okay," I said. "Anything else I need to know?"

"Yes. Apparently these guys are product investors and Brandon wants to show them results. He met with them today, and when they were done, he came out of the boardroom buzzing. He never once thought about the money some of the older guys could bring in, but this could be a game changer for Brand Nue."

"Does Brandon need a game changer?"

"He's got expenses, for sure. Running a business like this takes capital. His investors bailed after five consecutive years of posted losses. That's when he went all in."

Brandon needed money. But how did that relate back to Kyle's disappearance?

"Anything from Kyle?" I asked. "Any activity on his burner or posts to his feeds?"

"Yes. Didn't you hear? Kyle called in this morning. He apologized for being MIA and said he needed time to recover from the holiday party. His latest update is going nuts. Check it out when you get a chance. He even tagged you."

I thanked Rosha and grabbed my phone. A new post appeared in my feed. It was Kyle with bedhead, looking scruffy. He sat on the corner of his bed, dressed in a white T-shirt and black Adidas track pants with white stripes down the side. His eyes were covered by mirrored sunglasses, and his feet were bare.

Women would love this picture of him. Behind him was a tangle of white sheets on an unmade bed. Natural light from the window bathed him in a soft glow. On the nightstand, conveniently placed to display the product label, was a large bottle of the water we'd been hired to promote a few nights ago. Among Kyle's hashtags were #thehangover, #hangoverremedies, #dehydrationisnojoke, and #whereiskyletrent? and #sleepingitoff. By including the last two hashtags, he both asked and answered the question I'd posed to the world with my own hashtag campaign.

To anyone watching, Kyle's business was business as usual.

23

MAKEOVER

Was it possible I'd convinced a whole bunch of people to get on board a missing person case when the person in question had been sleeping off a wild party?

This jumping to conclusions thing of mine was getting out of hand. I'd said this time things would be different, but they were not. They were exactly as they'd been all along.

I commented on Kyle's post. "Good to have you rejoin the living!" with a heart, then backspaced over the words and left the heart on its own. Let his followers come up with their own theories about what it meant. People loved drawing conclusions and creating theories about our lives.

My burner vibrated on the table and I checked my texts. As promised, Rosha sent me the details for the Wrist Wrap party. I forwarded the texts to my personal phone—what did it matter if I violated company policy now?—and scanned the info, when the front door opened.

I looked up. Nick walked in, followed by two older men.

Two powerful looking older men. The first was Nick Senior. I'd first met him in Nick's shoe showroom over ten years ago—my first appointment anywhere as a shoe buyer. I mistakenly thought he was the Nick Taylor I was scheduled to meet with, an error he perpetuated because he liked having a joke at the new buyer's expense. The main reason the confusion worked was because Nick Senior had style. Even in office casual, as he'd been dressed that day, he looked like he belonged in the world of fashion. Since sustaining the injury that led him to move here and live with Nick, he'd shifted into sweats, but still, I knew he knew how to dress. Seeing him in a topcoat over a suit and tie was just an extension of the man I already knew.

It wasn't him that threw me off, it was the other guy.

As a lifelong lover of movies, I'm no stranger to the concept of a makeover. *Working Girl, Sabrina,* and *A Lowdown Dirty Shame* are among my favorites. In the movies, a successful makeover requires patience, time, and a team of experts.

I wanted to meet the experts who'd made over Detective Loncar.

When Loncar separated from his wife, his hair was the first to show signs of bachelorhood. The cut was uneven enough to suggest he'd done it himself. After that, he'd returned to a military buzz cut. An improvement, sure, but more suited to his crabby disposition than this new role as publicity client.

Tonight, his head had been shaved. It took years off his appearance. He wore a chocolate brown turtleneck under a camelhair topcoat and dark denim jeans over brown suede loafers.

I'd never seen Loncar's feet in loafers. I admit, I stared at them longer than was polite.

"You done checking me out yet?" he asked.

My head snapped up to his face. "I'm not checking you out." I blushed a little. Who knew Loncar had this in him?

"The cashiers at the coffee shop were checking him out," Nick Senior said. "This is great. I finally found a wingman." He passed the rest of us and walked over to the sofa where Logan sat.

As soon as I saw Logan, I remembered the puppy. I hadn't even thought about hiding the crate! Nick's surprise gift for his dad was about to go directly down the tubes.

On cue, the puppy whimpered. Nick looked at me. I looked at Nick Senior. Nick Senior looked at the crate. Slowly, he bent down and unlocked it. "Who's this?" he asked.

The black French bulldog came out and looked up at Nick Senior. Senior ran his hand over the puppy's head.

"She's looking for a home," Nick said. "I thought you might know of one."

Nick Senior looked up. "You got her for me?"

"Merry Christmas, Dad," Nick said.

I'd never tell a soul, but I'm pretty sure Loncar swiped tears from his eyes.

THE EVENT at Pop Shop was in full swing when Nick and I arrived. The interior had been transformed with close-up images of yarn. Fixtures knotted with Geri's colorful scarves were positioned around the shop, as were tables with champagne flutes, bottles of colorful soda, and bags of flavored popcorn. Brandon had gone with an inviting colorful, novelty shop vibe and judging from the line out front, people wanted to know what it was all about.

A crowd filled the interior, and a line of people waited to get in by the front door. I saw no familiar faces, which was both good and bad. If anybody I knew was there and they knew I shouldn't be, our—my—whole plan would be out the window.

The dress code said "cozy casual." I'd misinterpreted enough of these vague directions to stop caring if I got this one right. I wore a mint green down-filled puffy coat over mint green pants with white tuxedo stripes and white high-top sneakers from Saint Nick.

Okay, I cared a little.

Loncar and Nick Senior had planned to make a late appearance to check out the event. As investors, not designers, they wouldn't be expected to pose in pictures or mingle with the crowd. Their appearance would simply be to check out the event and see what Brand Nue could do for them. It was like an audition for future business.

What nobody but us knew was that they were waiting to hear from me. I was the eyes and ears on the inside, and right now, I had one job: get inside the party.

Except none of my team knew the truth. Kyle wasn't missing. Our rescue mission was a joke. For all I knew, he would show up at the party.

"You ready?" Nick asked. He held my hand and squeezed.

I held back. "Not yet. I think I need to reapply lip gloss."

"Don't you use a filter for that? Not that I'm a fan of those kinds of apps, but your contract said they were preloaded on your phone and you were supposed to make use of them."

"Kyle's not missing," I blurted. I sat very still, clutching Nick's hand. He relaxed his and slid his fingers away from mine.

"What?"

"Kyle's not missing," I repeated. "He was, and there were those scary posts, but he called Brand Nue today and said he was sleeping off a hangover. And he posted a selfie from his bedroom, and he's been responding to comments all day."

"Show me," Nick said.

I pulled out my personal phone and cued up Instagram. It took a bit of scrolling to find the picture of Kyle, but when I did, I handed my phone to Nick.

"His post has already been liked over two thousand times," I said. "His Instagram story, the one that cried out for help and the update with the screenshot, they felt like they were building up to something. That's how Brand Nue took it—that Kyle was prepping for an announcement or a mic drop. But this? It's anticlimactic, don't you think?"

"Kidd, we have a pretty elaborate sting going on tonight. You may have been the one to bring this to Loncar's attention, but he's not going to go to those great lengths on the word of somebody he—let's just say he thinks something's wrong here too. You're not making people do anything they don't want to do. This is either a party, or it's not. That's it."

"If it's not, then a lot of people are in danger."

"Are they? So far, Kyle's the only person who appeared to be in danger."

"I think he still is."

Nick held up my phone. "You just told me he's fine."

"Give me that."

Nick handed me the phone, and I stared at the image. I knew all the tricks that Brand

Nue had taught us. This picture didn't have to be real. It just had to look real. And it did. It looked *too* real.

That's what felt off to me.

I swiped down on Kyle's page, pausing at random to click on his images. Each one had a blurred background and slightly manipulated colors to unify the look of his so-called casual life pics. What had Candi told me? Brand Nue keeps a furnished townhouse for the influencers to use. That must be where these pictures were taken.

I scrolled back to the latest pic, the one that said he'd been sleeping off a hangover. Unlike the previous ones, this hadn't been run through a filter. The background was sharp, and I easily noticed items scattered around the room that would otherwise have been blurry. A pair of sneakers peeking out from under the bed. Some jeans sat crumpled on the floor. These were the details that people loved. A window into how Kyle lives. But if this were a furnished townhouse, then would he really have his clothes strewn around? Would he sleep off the party there or in his own home?

There was something else about the picture that bothered me. The sunglasses. If he really wanted to block the sun, he'd close the blinds. And taking a selfie by remote camera with mirrored glasses wasn't a great idea, because the equipment would be reflected on the lens.

How did I not think of that sooner?

I tapped the picture and used my fingers to magnify it. As suspected, there was a reflection on the lens of Kyle's aviators. It wasn't photo equipment. It was a woman taking his picture with a cell phone.

And it wasn't just any woman, either. With her platinum blond hair tied up in little nubs across her head, she was easily recognizable. It was Rosha, the receptionist from Brand Nue.

The one who told me Kyle was missing.

The one who told me Kyle was back.

24

ACCESS TO EVERYTHING

"It's Rosha," I said.

"Where?"

"In the reflection of Kyle's glasses. She's the one who took this picture."

"Who's Rosha?"

"The receptionist at Brand Nue. She's Brandon's right hand person." I examined the image again. Now that I knew what I was looking for, there was no missing it. "She sought me out in the lobby the day I was there and told me she was worried about Kyle. She said she was out of town at a family gig in

Jersey the night he went missing, and I believed her. She has access to everything at the company: the tracking info, the burner phone feeds, the assignments, and the schedules. She knows where we are when we're there and what we're doing."

I set the phone in my lap and stared out the window. "She's the one who told me to come here tonight."

"Yes, but that's your assignment. She gave you all your jobs, right?"

I turned to look at Nick. "I was let go tonight. Brandon fired me. He said the best influencers gloss over the details and make things look good at face value, but I was too concerned with digging below the surface to expose the truth. He said I'm a natural investigator and that's the opposite of being an influencer."

Nick put his arm around me. "You've been waiting for someone to acknowledge your natural investigative skills for years. Did you tell Loncar?"

"Not yet."

"Can I be there when you do?"

I smiled. "Sure."

As cozy as it was sitting in the cab of Nick's truck in the parking lot outside Pop Shop, I couldn't ignore what I'd figured out. If Rosha was behind Kyle's disappearance, then Kyle might still be missing. Who knew when that picture had been taken. Or where. Or why.

I called Loncar. He answered on the first ring. I plunged into the conversation without giving him a moment to talk. "Hi. Can you hear me? I have to tell you some stuff. You don't have to answer, just let me know you heard me. Okay?"

"Ms. Kidd. I'm in my car outside Brand Nue. I can speak freely."

"Okay, but that's not important. This is. Brandon Nue's receptionist is the one who kidnapped Kyle. I haven't worked out why yet, but as of tonight she's trying to make it seem like he's fine and has been sleeping off a hangover."

"Where is he?"

"I don't know." I told him about Rosha's reflection in Kyle's sunglasses, about how she controlled his social media feeds, and my lack of access to the event. "The company keeps a furnished apartment around here somewhere."

"It's across the street from the office," Loncar said.

"How do you know that?"

"It was in your contract. I'm about to check it out."

"You're going to break in, aren't you?" Loncar didn't say anything. "You're going to pick the locks. You are so much cooler as a PI than you were as a cop."

"Ms. Kidd, if your suspicions are correct, then this is dangerous work. I can't provide protection like I could when I was on the police force. Take precautions, and if you feel at any time you are in over your head, get out. Do I make myself clear?"

"Crystal."

I hung up and clutched my phone. Other things fell into place. If Rosha was guilty, then Candi and Leon were not. Candi's insistence that something was wrong made her my first phone call. "It's Samantha," I said when she answered. "Did you see?"

"Kyle didn't take that f***in' picture."

"I know. Listen—did you get an assignment to work at Pop Shop tonight? A last-minute client?"

"Yeah. I said I'd try to make it, but I thought tonight was a free night. I'm having dinner in f***in' Philly right now, so if I do make it, it'll be late. Why?"

"I can't get into details, but Brandon let me go today and I lost access."

"Where you at?" she asked. "Location

finder says you're there."

I'd forgotten to disable the Find Me app. If Rosha was monitoring my whereabouts, she'd think I was here. I could use this. But one phone call to Brandon would ruin everything.

"Candi, I gotta go. Enjoy your dinner."

I hung up and turned to Nick. "Anybody who has a Brand Nue phone can see that I'm here. I forgot to turn off location finder and Rosha could be tracking me."

"You can't go in there," he correctly stated.

"Right. But my phone can."

"Easy problem to solve." Nick shifted his eyes from my face to my phone. He leaned away from me and held the pocket of his overcoat open. I dropped my burner phone in. "It's cold out. Go sit in the car and keep the engine running."

I watched Nick until he disappeared around the corner of the building. Something we'd reasoned out stuck with me. For the past two weeks, I'd been living the high life all expenses paid at party after party, on bills footed by clients who wanted publicity. The pictures Kyle and I took at these parties were a fraction of what turned up with the designated hashtags. I could search through the background of any number of images, not just those from Brand Nue, and get an idea of what these parties were like. If you weren't on social media like Eddie, then you'd hate these events. Everywhere you went, a camera would snap a picture. You'd have to exist in a controlled environment to avoid showing up in a background.

It was at that moment that I realized where Kyle was being held. I moved from the passenger side of the truck to the driver's side and peeled out of my parking space. Nick would be as safe as a baby in a room filled with kittens.

Detective Loncar was the one in danger.

25

A CAPER

Rosha never worked in the field and she rarely left the office. That told me two things: she wouldn't accidentally be photographed in the background of a party pic, and wherever she was holding Kyle, it was close to Brand Nue. She wouldn't risk letting him be out of her sight for long.

I drove as fast as the weather would allow. Rosha had an edge on me with the tracking software and whatever I'd agreed to in that contract, but she only knew what she knew. Meaning it was time to go old school.

Phase one: I needed a team who couldn't be found.

I called Eddie. "Yo," I said. "You up for a caper?"

"Dude, I'm still in Florida."

"I was hoping you'd say that." I gave him an update and outlined my plan. Eddie was, as expected, eager to help. He agreed to call in favors from friends from around the country. If he could get them to do the same, we'd have a real-live ghost-to-ghost hookup in minutes.

I left him to coordinate a social media blitz of our fake company from his remote location while I cut the lights and parked on a side street near Brand Nue. Faint light glowed from a window on the third floor. It could be Loncar, skulking about with a pen light, searching through Brand Nue's files.

Or it could be Rosha.

My request to Eddie had been simple. Style a series of product photos and coordinate a social media blitz using the hashtags we'd been assigned for Geri's company. The idea was to impact the efforts of the Brand Nue influencers and force Brandon's hand in examining the autonomy he gave Rosha. Brandon would be monitoring the hashtag from the party, and at first sign of other hashtags watering down the feed, he would respond swiftly. Rosha would go into problem-solving mode, leaving us free for a rescue mission.

If I were right. All of this was contingent upon me being right.

I reminded myself that an anonymous donor had recently paid me a quarter of a million dollars for following my hunch and being right. It was of little consolation.

I swiped my keycard against the pad on the back door and the locks clunked open. That was encouraging. Brandon may have fired me, but he hadn't cut off my access. Knowing what I did about Brandon's security cameras recording the elevator wells, I searched the main floor for the exit signs, went through the door below one, and found the emergency stairs. I'd never been so happy to be wearing sneakers.

It was three floors up before I reached Brand Nue, and nothing about my lifestyle put me in the kind of shape where I wasn't out of breath. I stood on in the stairwell and waited for my heartbeat to calm down.

The door to the stairwell swung open. If I'd been on the other side of the door, I would have been hidden behind it. As is, I was so startled I almost fell down the stairs.

Rosha aimed a penlight directly at my eyes. I blinked rapidly. She clicked the light off and bursts of blue and magenta blobs clouded my vision. "Come on in," she said. "I've been expecting you."

26

NOT HIS KEEPER

I WAS FILLED WITH CONJECTURE AND UNSPOKEN accusations, but this wasn't like other cases I'd been involved with. As far as I knew, Kyle was still alive. Depending on what Rosha wanted, the way things played out tonight could have an impact on that fact.

"How'd you know I was there?" I asked.

"This place is covered in cameras and not solely for security. These stairwells were the perfect backdrop for a series of images for a local streetwear company. Brandon brought in a graffiti artist to do the backdrop. A little paint goes a long way around here."

"It's one thing if you have models staging a campaign, but another to take pictures without consent."

"You still don't get it, do you? The money that passes through these doors? Our clients don't care about privacy in elevator wells and staircases. They pay for results. Kyle said you had good instincts, but I don't think you're good enough at this kind of work to go freelance."

"Where is he?" I asked.

"This again? I told you. He was sleeping off a hangover. You saw the post on his Instagram feed."

I yanked my arm away from her. "I saw your reflection in his mirrored sunglasses too. You took that picture. Kyle didn't."

She sighed. "Kyle likes to party. Hard. It works with his image, so Brandon tolerates it. When Kyle starts missing work, it becomes a problem. I took that picture so it wouldn't become a problem."

"Where is he now?"

"How should I know? I'm not his keeper."

We were standing inside the lobby of Brand Nue, not far from where Leon had confronted Brandon. I couldn't believe it was the same day that had happened.

"But you are, Rosha. You're all of our keepers. You know where we go and what we do. You see what we post, and you pay us our fees. You're the real mastermind here, not Brandon. You probably already know he fired me earlier today, but for some reason, you wanted me to think you didn't."

"Of course, I knew. Brandon told me to deactivate your keycard as soon as you left him at Pop Shop."

"Why didn't you?"

"Because I figured if something were to happen, you'd make a good scapegoat. You, Leon, Candi, take your pick. Every one of you is interchangeable. You take your pictures and post your hashtags, but you have no idea the story is written by me. I'm the one who tells you where to go, what to say, how to dress."

She was becoming bolder, but so far she hadn't said anything incriminating. I needed her to crack. I needed her to make a mistake. "Kyle's not dead yet, right? Because if he is, that's a different crime. Brandon might trust you to research hashtags, but do you really think he's going to let you drag his company into a possible murder investigation? I may not be cut out for influencer work, but I know about criminal activities." I stepped toward her and she stepped back. That was a good sign. She was afraid of me. "I know about the cops. I know they're on their way right now."

"The cops are investigating the townhouse across the street. I called in an anonymous tip. They'll find Kyle's DNA, but they'll also find everybody else's. That should confuse the investigators for a while.

Kyle had been missing for less than twenty-four hours. Too early for a missing person's case. If the police were investigating anything, it was a routine disturbance call, not a full-on forensic team prepared to collect evidence. I knew that, but there had been a time when I didn't. When everything I knew about police work came from TV and movies. And if Rosha thought she was in control, then I'd run with it.

"If there's even a whiff of criminal activity happening in this building, there's only one way for Brandon to deal with it. Hang you out to dry. And I'm guessing he'd do it publicly. I mean, he does have this place wired with cameras. I'm sure he can dig up something to incriminate you."

"You were fired earlier today. You're a trespasser on company property. I'm calling the police," she said.

"Go ahead," I said, calling her bluff. "According to you, they're in the neighborhood." I even picked up the burner phone that lay on her desk and offered it to her.

She looked down at the phone. It was like every other burner phone they'd given the influencers. I waited for her to take it. She stared at it as though that phone signified something.

I turned the phone toward me and pressed the home button. Nothing happened. I held down the power button and the image of an empty battery showed up for a moment and then vanished. The phone went back to black.

"It's dead," Rosha said.

She remained tense. There was something about this phone that made her nervous. Something she didn't want me to find. I set it on the charging base and stepped between the desk and her. If she wanted it, she'd have to go through me.

"I know you know what happened to Kyle," I said. "You're responsible for his disappearance. Whatever you did, wherever you're hiding him, you won't get away with it."

"You have no evidence. You can't prove anything."

There was nothing keeping Rosha from leaving Brand Nue. She could have made a break for it at any time. If she did, she'd probably get away and I still wouldn't know where Kyle was.

But she stayed.

The phone lit up. Rosha and I noticed the glowing screen at the same time. She lunged for it, but I grabbed it and held it out of reach. Rosha's eyes were wild. Two of the small knots of hair on the top of her head had come undone, leaving weird tufts of hair standing on end in patches.

I keyed in the universal lock code and checked the battery usage. In the last twenty-four hours, the only apps that had been used were photos and Instagram.

This was an influencer phone. I opened

Instagram and saw Kyle's face peering back at me. Was it enough proof that Rosha had Kyle's burner? Probably not. It belonged to Brand Nue. There were any number of reasons for it to be here.

I cued up the photos and there it was. The evidence I was looking for.

The most recent photo was a blurry image of a woman bending over a wooden crate. The picture was blurry, but there was no mistaking the spiky blond hair knotted on top of her head or the piercings through her eyebrow and nose.

Gotcha.

And then Rosha did something unmistakable. She stepped backward and put her hand on the third crate of the stack. Not the top one. Not the one closest to her, but the one that had been sitting there since the day Leon was there. There was something different about that crate. The others were sealed. That one was not. One could argue that it had air holes, and I knew why.

“I’ll give you half the money,” Rosha said. “Seventy-five grand wired to your bank account. That’s more money than most people make in a year.”

“That’s all this was about?” I asked. “Money?”

“Money is everything. It’s the only thing. Be careful, Samantha. Spend enough time in this world and you’ll start to believe some hot new product can change your life, but it can’t. There’s only one thing that can.”

“Money won’t change your life either,” I said. “I’ve got a quarter of a million dollars in the bank right now and nothing’s different.”

And in that moment, I realized how wonderful that was. I didn’t want things to be different. I didn’t want things to change. I wanted my friends to be my friends and rely on me because they knew they could. I wanted to love Nick and know he loved me back, not because I found him the perfect Christmas present, but because of me. I wanted Loncar to keep challenging me when I jumped to conclusions and forcing me to think things through. I wanted pizza to be my favorite dinner and pretzels to be my favorite snack and Logan to be my favorite cat. I wanted "Money Changes Everything" to be a song by Cyndi Lauper, not a belief system.

"It's been awhile since Kyle posted anything to Instagram. It's time for an update, don't you think?"

With one hand, I launched Instagram, selected the most recent photo, and posted it without comment or hashtag. Seconds later, notifications started pouring in. Kyle's followers were on it.

So was Detective Loncar. Not a minute went by before he burst through the door with a handful of police. Thanks to the Find Me app, they'd been there all along.

27

LOOSE ENDS

We found Kyle, unconscious, in one of the crates. He was dressed in the outfit on his recent Instagram post: white T-shirt, black Adidas pants, bare feet. Rosha sat him in a chair and then photoshopped him into a picture taken in the townhouse.

Loncar was quick to point out the clean soles of Kyle's bare feet. He'd learned on his walkthrough of the townhouse that new carpeting had been installed, and a film of fibers clung to the soles and heels of his new shoes. Had he been wearing his usual orthopedic style he never would have noticed the transfer of carpet fibers. #NewShoesRule!

There were a couple of winners that emerged from the debacle. Geri Loncar, who'd struggled to sell her hand-knit scarves and took a job managing her dad's PI business, sold out of her inventory and took orders for more. It wasn't the representation of Loncar and Nick Senior that made the difference, it was Eddie. The campaign he launched with our designated hashtags drew attention to the party and the trend took off. I suspected Eddie would have a job offer from Wrist Wraps before he returned home.

Nick and I spent the holidays at home with his dad, Logan, and the French Bulldog. There were too many pretzels, too much wine, numerous holiday movies, and frequent naps. His dad and the French Bulldog, who was still nameless, joined us for the Taylor family annual viewing of *Die Hard.* Who was I to argue with tradition?

As for Kyle, he spent Christmas in the hospital recovering from extreme dehydration and fatigue. The doctors said there would be no long-term damage and he'd be back to his old self with rest and a proper diet. Candi kept him company while he recovered, arriving selfie-ready every day until he was released.

The story broke, as was to be expected, on social media.

BONUS! MADISON NIGHT HOLIDAY FLASH FICTION STORY

WHEN I FIRST TOLD MY FRIENDS, CLIENTS, AND employees that I wanted to host a holiday party at Mad for Mod, I was met with enthusiasm—for five seconds. And then planners and phones came out, schedules were checked, and the grumbling began. How is it people who complain year-long that their lives have become boring are suddenly overbooked with party after party from organization after organization?

I nixed the idea of a party. Still, I have a metal file cabinet filled with vintage ornaments, and a little decorating never hurt anybody.

"Hey, Madison? Here's that box of vintage ornaments from the storage locker." I took the proffered box from Effie Jones, my full-time millennial employee. I was teaching her about the mid-century modern aesthetic, and she was teaching me about Slack, integrated mailing lists, and Zoom. She brought up King Sumo last week, and I told her unless he came with gold, frankincense, or myrrh, I wasn't ready to meet him. (Apparently, he didn't.)

I took the ornaments, spun them one at a time like a grocery store shopper inspecting a carton for broken eggs, and handed them back to her. "Connie and Mitchell are almost done setting up the Evergleam Pom-Pom trees. You can do the honors of placing the Christmas balls if you want."

"Isn't that a big job?" Effie asked. Her eyes widened, and for a moment she looked like the introverted college student she'd been when I first met her.

"Two days ago you automated my mailing list and placed a tracking pixel on my website."

"That was easy."

"Effie, I think you can handle some Christmas balls."

She relaxed. "Whatever you say, boss."

I watched as my friends laughed and decorated. It was 7:15 a.m. We hadn't been able to coordinate party schedules, but when they heard I was going to decorate early today, they showed up one by one without being asked.

There was Connie, a recently separated former employee who now worked in a niche aspect of the record industry, stringing twinkle lights around the perimeter of the showroom.

Mitchell, manager of Paintin' Place, the store where I frequently shopped and occasionally endorsed products.

Joanie, owner of Joanie Loves Tchotchkes, a thrift store that often sold me items I could have gotten for free if I'd woken up five minutes earlier and beaten Joanie to the dumpster on trash day.

Rocky, my caramel and white Shih-Tzu, had been outfitted with tiny reindeer horns and bells and ran around the shop yipping at the activity.

Effie, who you already know.

One person was missing. One person who—

The front door chimes jingled and Santa Claus walked in with a bottle of Veuve Cliquot in each hand and a jug of orange juice under his elbow. "Ho, ho, ho," he said. Instantly I knew his costume was vintage—a soft, red velour trimmed with white fur that was as fluffy as his beard. The square patent-leather buckle, the drape of the trousers, and the boots—shiny black riding boots that Clint

Walker could have worn in Send Me No Flowers.

This could not be happening. Santa Claus had more important things to do than come to my showroom at 7:15 and deliver mimosas.

We locked eyes and a warm feeling coursed through me. I felt myself blush from the tips of my shiny red patent leather kitten heels, under my ivory double-knit polyester shift dress with the red daisies embroidered at the empire waist, and all the way to the top of the ivory turtleneck I'd worn underneath.

"Merry Christmas," Santa said. He wiggled the bottles and waggled his eyebrows. "You like?"

"This didn't come from Amazon," I said.

"No. I called around and found it at a costume shop in Nevada called Disguise DeLimit. The owner said it's from 1964."

I joined him and considered giving him a thank you peck on the cheek, but all that white synthetic hair was a little off-putting. "I thought you had an important meeting this morning?"

"Going to visit the local elementary school. I thought I'd stop here first."

"So this," I gestured up and down Santa Claus's outfit, "is for them? Not me?"

He stroked his beard. "Well, for now, yes, it's for them." He grinned. I took the bottles and juice and watched Santa wave to my elves and then turn to the door. He stopped and turned back. "Yo, Night." I rented the vintage Mrs. Claus costume too. It's in the back seat. You want to join me?"

"I tell you what. You handle the grade school. I'll handle the workshop. But tonight..."

Santa Claus's eyes darkened. "Tonight?"

"Tonight it'll just be you and me..."

...and it was. Unfortunately, the early morning, day-with-the-elementary-school-children, and decorating marathon had an unfortunate effect on both of us. We fell asleep (in our vintage Santa and Mrs. Claus costumes) before nine o'clock that night.

Note to self: call Disguise DeLimit and extend the rental. After all, it's only December 6th.

Want a bonus ebook that you can't get anywhere else? Join the Weekly DiVa Club and receive BONBONS FOR YOUR BRAIN, a collection of humorous essays about everything from writing mysteries to buying shoes to being the best version of yourself. Get the offer at dianevallere.com/weekly-diva.

ABOUT THE AUTHOR

National bestselling author Diane Vallere writes smart, funny, and fashionable character-based mysteries. After two decades working for a top luxury retailer, she traded fashion accessories for accessories to murder. A past president of Sisters in Crime, Diane started her own detective agency at age ten and has maintained a passion for shoes, clues, and clothes ever since. Find out more at dianevallere.com.

ALSO BY

Samantha Kidd Mysteries

Designer Dirty Laundry

Buyer, Beware

The Brim Reaper

Some Like It Haute

Grand Theft Retro

Pearls Gone Wild

Cement Stilettos

Panty Raid

Union Jacked

Slay Ride

Tough Luxe

Fahrenheit 501

Stark Raving Mod

Madison Night Mad for Mod Mysteries

"Midnight Ice" (prequel novella)

Pillow Stalk

That Touch of Ink

With Vics You Get Eggroll

The Decorator Who Knew Too Much

The Pajama Frame

Lover Come Hack

Apprehend Me No Flowers

Teacher's Threat

The Kill of it All

Sylvia Stryker Outer Space Mysteries

Fly Me To The Moon

I'm Your Venus

Saturn Night Fever

Spiders from Mars

Material Witness Mysteries

Suede to Rest

Crushed Velvet

Silk Stalkings

<u>Costume Shop Mystery Series</u>

A Disguise to Die For

Masking for Trouble

Dressed to Confess

www.ingramcontent.com/pod-product-compliance
Lightning Source LLC
Chambersburg PA
CBHW030417310726
48979CB00002B/449

* 9 7 8 1 9 5 4 5 7 9 7 1 2 *